SUPERNATURAL BOUNTY HUNTER

MAGIC TOUCH BOOK 3

LEIA STONE & LUCÍA ASHTA

This book is a work of fiction.

Cover design by Mirela Barbu.

Edited by Lee Burton.

ISBN 978-1-0793-9235-7
July 2019

Learn about Leia and Lucía's books at
LeiaStone.com and LuciaAshta.com.

To Cass, the best bestie ever.
Your booty shorts rock.
We only wish you were real!

1 THIS SHIT'S OFFICIAL

MOLLY STRUTTED up and down the length of Brock's wraparound porch gesturing to her brand-spanking-new shiny Bounty Hunter Apprentice badge clipped on her hip. "Take a real good look, guys. This shit's official!" she boomed, her wide smile taking up most of her face. We all whistled and cheered her on. Tianna, Reo, and Haru heckled her, but you could see the delight on their faces. They were damn proud.

Cass and I shared a grin.

'Took me two times to pass my apprentice test,' my bestie said. *'I'm proud of our girl.'*

I chuckled. Cass wasn't the best with written tests, and the proctor had been a fae who'd distracted him, directing his thoughts straight to hanky-panky.

'I'm proud of her too.'

Molly getting officially badged was a bright spot in an otherwise dark week. After Calista and her bitch siren sister disappeared into the underworld, I'd barely slept. Any day now they could march through with their army and try to enslave humanity. Brock posted a handful of wolves at the gate to the underworld at all times, with instructions to kill whatever came out of it and call us. Still, this was my destiny or whatever, which made it difficult to pass off the responsibility.

Haru and Reo said I'd need all nine tails in order to close the gate, and even then they didn't know exactly how I'd manage it since I was a hybrid. Only a kitsune could permanently seal the gate, and I was only half kitsune, half witch. Nothing about the situation was ideal. In fact, everything about the clusterfuck we currently found ourselves in was as far from ideal as it got. Humanity's survival hung in the balance, and we were figuring it out on the fly.

My dad was MIA, and I'd only shifted one time in the week since Calista and her sister disappeared into the gate —three more times to go. My new power: enhanced hearing. I could hear heartbeats, which was cool, but it also made it hard to sleep. Brock's and the baby's heartbeats pounded in my head all night long, when I needed my rest more than ever. Shifter pregnancies were accelerated. Gestation lasted a total of six months instead of nine, which meant this baby was going to be popping out of me in ten weeks or so—ready or not. Brock was trying to teach me to not focus on the sound of their beating hearts, but I was struggling. In truth, I was struggling to adjust to many aspects of my new crazy-as-fuck life, but fate hadn't bothered to ask my opinion on the matter.

Brock sidled up to where I leaned against the porch railing to whisper in my ear. "Sabine is here."

Today we were going to find out the sex of the baby. Brock was trying to act neutral, but I knew he was dead set on a boy, so the universe would probably give us a girl to spite him. I couldn't think of a single thing that had gone to plan since Brock and I first met.

I gave Cass a nervous smile and pushed off from the railing. "I'll be back in a bit," I told Molly. "Remember, if you screw anything up, that badge gets taken."

She saluted me. "Yes, ma'am. Have a good ultrasound, ma'am."

Little shit. I grabbed a loose grape from the nearby picnic table and chucked it at her face. Laughing, she dodged it easily, which only caused my grin to grow wider. Molly had become like a little sister to me. I'd moved in with Brock just last night, after Molly signed a lease on Gran's cabin. I was renting it to her for ten dollars a month. That's about all she could afford. Hopefully, having a place of her own would keep her from blood-whoring with Croft. I liked the vamp attorney well enough, and I loved that he was the new head of the local seethe of vampires. But I didn't want him to keep draining my dear friend of blood. She was always pale and shaky for a good while after his visits, and I'd had enough of that. Besides, her little ménage with Reo and Haru seemed to be going well. The brothers stayed at the cabin with her. Every night. All together.

You go, girl.

Brock laced his fingers through mine and led me back to our shared bedroom. The first thing I'd done was bring over all of Gran's witchy shit. I'd placed it sporadically around Brock's place, partially because I needed the stuff and enjoyed the constant reminders of the one woman who'd loved me when no one else had, and partially to test how much Brock loved me. So far, even though werewolves in general had an aversion to witches and their gear, he hadn't said a word or raised an eyebrow. The man was total perfection.

"I was thinking teal for the nursery, with a mountain-scape hand-painted by a local artist. If it's a boy, of course," he told me as we walked into the room.

"Sounds good. And if it's a girl, no mermaids."

Brock chuckled, giving me a sexy grin. "Agreed. Not even a hint of one. We can tell the artist to leave out water entirely."

"You guys ready to find out the sex of the baby?" Sabine asked as she fiddled with some settings on her portable ultrasound machine.

Brock cringed. "The words sex and baby shouldn't be used in the same sentence."

Sabine rolled her eyes. "Fine. Gender."

I waved them both off. "We're beyond ready. Brock is already talking about hiring local artists to paint the nursery."

Sabine grinned and pulled out the wand as I kicked off my boots, lay down on the bed, and inched down the waistband of my maternity pants. Yep, I'd graduated to the elastic band stuff. Cass teased me mercilessly about the new additions to my wardrobe, but coming from an imp who shopped in the toddler section of stores ... I wasn't very offended.

My belly was pretty prominent considering I was past the halfway point of the pregnancy. I couldn't deny it anymore.

I. Was. Knocked. Up.

Sabine squirted cold gel on my belly and brought the wand down over my bellybutton. I was so grateful to have graduated from the internal dildo ultrasound. That wasn't fun for anyone.

Brock sat on the bed on my other side and leaned forward, watching the blobs on the screen like a hawk and clutching my hand like it was a life raft and we were lost at sea.

I used our pack bond to speak: *'Chill out a little. I can't feel my fingers.'*

He immediately let up on my hand and grinned. *'I'm just so excited.'*

Brock's excitement for our baby was one of my favorite things about him. The world was falling to shit, psychotic mermaids were probably about to lead a demon hoard onto earth to slaughter us all, but Brock was ready to paint the nursery.

"Hmm." Sabine pushed the ultrasound wand into my stomach a little more firmly than usual.

"What's wrong?" Brock's every muscle bunched as he scrambled to stand, ready to fight whatever was ailing our baby.

Sabine looked at her alpha. "Nothing. I just can't see the sex, er, gender. Little baby has its umbilical cord between its legs, and those legs are crossed."

Brock let out the breath he'd been holding, and I burst into a fit of giggles. When he looked over at me, eyebrows raised in question, I grabbed his arm. "Maybe we shouldn't know. Let it be a surprise." I was a total control freak and normally hated surprises, but this sounded kind of fun.

Brock ignored me and faced Sabine, staring at the screen. "That's a penis. It's a boy!" He pointed excitedly to a dangling blob.

Sabine chuckled. "Seriously, that's the umbilical cord. You're going to have to wait until next week."

His whole face fell.

"Or we could let it be a surprise…" I offered again.

He looked back at me with amber eyes. "No. If I'm having a daughter, I need to mentally prepare."

My jaw dropped. "What the fuck is that supposed to mean?"

Sabine cleared her throat. "That's my cue to leave. Baby looks healthy. We'll do this again next week. You can shift one more time. Baby seems to be handling it okay."

Sabine was tracking the shifts that were sprouting new tails and granting me more powers and how it was all affecting the baby. We were so far into uncharted territory that we weren't even on the map.

I just nodded, anxious for her to leave Brock and me alone. He had some major mansplaining to do.

The second Sabine was out of ear shot, Brock grumbled, "You're taking this the wrong way."

I wiped the gel from my stomach in choppy movements, yanked down my shirt, and crossed my arms to glare at him. "Explain yourself. I will not have a child with a sexist alpha whatever you are."

Brock grinned. "Sexist alpha whatever…"

"Explain." I kicked my legs over the edge of the bed and started tugging on my boots.

Brock reached out and stilled me, cupping my face. "You're the most beautiful woman I've ever laid eyes on."

The breath whooshed out of me, and I couldn't help but stare up into those honey eyes of his.

"And if our daughter has even half of your beauty and a quarter of your feisty independence, I'll need to put bars on all the windows and have a tracking device implanted in her neck because the boys will be lining up for miles and my heart can't take it."

I grinned. "It's still sexist, but since that's pretty fucking sweet, I guess you're off the hook."

"Hmm, that's good, because I have better plans for that pout of yours." He edged between my legs, parting them.

"Oh, do you?"

"Definitely." He tilted my face up and lowered his lips toward mine. Right away, his tongue urged my lips apart; heat rushed across my body as our tongues met. I stood and he wrapped his arms around me, pulling me against him. Weaving my hands around his neck, I claimed his mouth. He kissed me like it was the first time and the last time, all at once. And even though we'd already made love that morning, I couldn't help the moan that escaped me and the way every part of my body urged me along, wanting more, more, more of this gorgeous man.

Brock groaned and cupped my ass, pressing my pelvis against his, convincing me that there was no such thing as too much sex. I'd never get enough of this man.

"Boy or girl, I'll be thrilled, I promise," he whispered against my lips, sending shivers vibrating down the length of my body.

I was two seconds away from tossing him onto the bed when someone banged on the door to the bedroom. I hadn't even realized Sabine had pulled it shut, but it was no secret in the house of wolves with acute hearing that Brock and I ended up between the sheets more often than not. She must have closed it to afford us privacy.

"Go away!" Brock ordered, trailing his fingertips across my collarbone like an erotic whisper.

"Evie! Get out here!" Cass yelled, and I froze in Brock's arms, whipping my face toward the closed door.

'*What is it?*' I broadcasted through the link Cass and I shared as I crossed the room and jerked the door open, looking down.

My two-foot-tall bounty hunting partner looked pale as a ghost. As a hot pink demon imp, this was hard to accomplish.

He swallowed visibly. "Your dad's here."

2 DADDY SAY WHAT?

'*DO you want me to tell him you're resting? Give you a little time to prepare?*'

Brock's compassionate offer snapped me out of my daze, and I blinked at him a few times as I came back to myself. Leaning my shoulder against the archway of our bedroom, I took a deep breath. Just down this hall was a large seating area where my father, the one whom I'd believed dead for most of my life, was waiting. Cass had already gone ahead of us, leaving Brock and me alone.

Brock brought a hand to the small of my back, his flesh warm against mine. '*I'm sure he'd understand...*'

A heavy sigh escaped me. I was a supernatural bounty hunter, for fuck's sake. I'd faced down more nasty creatures than I could count. I could do this. *Of course I can.* So what if I had no real memories of him or my mother before the car accident that supposedly killed them both? He was still my father ... everything would be fine ... it might just take a little time to get used to having a parent around.

When Gran passed, I'd felt orphaned, without family. Sure, I had Cass before Brock came along with Molly and the rest of my crazy crew. But my dad was … my dad.

My heart thumped uncomfortably in my chest, so loudly I could hear it, protesting my discomfort. What would he be like? Would we have things to talk about? Would he feel like a stranger? Other than the small conversation we'd had on the phone when I'd done that spell to trick the killing curse into thinking Nathan was me, we'd never spoken.

'Eve?' Brock tried again, massaging his hand against my back, and I shook my head, my long, dark hair scattering.

'Thanks, but I'm okay. He's my dad.' I stumbled over the word that I wasn't used to using. *Dad.* I'd dreamed of having parents for so long … this didn't seem possible. Why was I so freaked out when it's all I'd wanted for as long as I could remember?

Before I could mind-fuck myself more, I straightened my shoulders, flung my hair back, and tugged my crop-top down, though it was no use since my growing belly pushed the fabric right back up under my breasts. With total confidence, I marched through the archway—and froze mid-step when I first caught sight of him.

He looked so much like me—or rather I looked so much like him. He shared my straight, shiny black hair, oval face, and bright bow-like lips. The only striking difference were the violet eyes I'd gotten from my mother, though even the almond shape of them were like his.

I resumed my approach as he pinned his gaze on me, gesturing to a woman who stood behind him to roll his wheelchair so he'd meet me halfway.

"Hello, kitten," he said, and my heart seized for a moment.

"Hey, Father. Dad..." I struggled with what to call him.

The face that resembled mine creased into a gentle, warm smile, and I all but ran toward him. He opened his arms, and I leaned over to embrace him, doing my best not to focus on the fact that he was in a wheelchair. The fucking Akuma, or whoever had tried to kill him, had left him paralyzed and my mother dead. I was going to kill the next Akuma I saw.

He patted me awkwardly on the back. "I've longed to see you for so many years."

Pulling back, I stood in front of him. "Why are you here now? I mean, I'm so glad you're here, but ... why now? I thought it was dangerous for you to come here?" I scanned the spacious room. It was empty beyond Cass, my father, and the woman behind him, who looked like a caretaker.

He grimaced and rubbed at his chest, seemingly unconsciously. "The Akuma found me. I fear they'll find you next."

Feeling awkward towering over him, I took a seat on the nearest couch, thankful for Brock's support when he sank into the leather cushions beside me.

"Actually," I said, "they did find me. At a selkie cove I went to in order to heal my blade."

Understanding sparked in his eyes before turning to anger, and then melting into a fearful expression. "Then we have less time to complete your training than I thought."

Great. That sounded ominous.

Brock took my hand and leaned forward. "Hello, sir. I'm Brock. Welcome to our home."

My father's loving gaze traveled between us, across our linked hands, before he nodded once, his smile suddenly tight. "Thank you for having me." Then his gaze went to my belly. "Have you just had a large meal Evie, or am I going to become a grandfather?"

"Oh! Right." I giggled nervously. "We're expecting..." I let my admission linger because what the fuck else was I supposed to say to the dad I'd known for all of five minutes?

"This is your husband?" my father asked me, looking again between Brock and me. "Did I miss the wedding?"

A nervous shrill of laughter bubbled out of me before I inhaled sharply and choked on my own spit. A hacking cough had me in its clutches while Cass grinned like an idiot behind my father, clearly enjoying my discomfort.

"No. Brock isn't my husband, no. Just my baby daddy."

Oh fuck. Did I just say *baby daddy* in front of my father? Why were my palms sweating so much?

My father nodded, his expression completely blank and unreadable. "I see. So you intend to raise the child ... together ... but unwed?"

Fuck. Fuck. Fuck. Red alert. I needed out of this conversation, stat. What was even happening right now?

'Pull the fire alarm,' I told Cass.

His grin widened. *'This isn't school. No fire alarm. You just gotta deal with it.'*

Brock had tensed beside me, and I squeezed his hand in reassurance, for my sake as much as his. "Yes," I replied. "As I'm not married, our child will be born to unmarried parents."

Keep it cool, Evie. He's just trying to get to know you.

"I see," my father said again. "You have no plans to marry, then?"

Why was he having such a hard time grasping the situation? Anyway, weren't we just talking about the Akuma? How had the conversation turned so quickly?

'Do something or I'll never forgive you,' I told Cass, who was red faced, clutching his little potbelly, trying to hold in his laughter.

"No—" I was saying when Brock interrupted me.

"My intention has always been to marry your daughter, sir."

Say what? My eyebrows hit my hairline and my heart did all sorts of crazy somersaults in my chest. I was sure I wasn't containing my shock.

"I see that this is news to my daughter," my father said, and a hint of gentle amusement entered his tone.

But I ignored him for now, turned fully to face Brock. *'You planned to ... marry me?'*

Brock's eyes twinkled. *'What did you think I meant when I said I loved you and move in with me?'* He chuckled at our private conversation. *'You look as shocked as you did when you first found out you were pregnant.'*

'Well, yeah.' There was so much more I could say, but the words weren't quite forming. I sought out Cass instead. He would understand. He'd known me long before my life threatened to get all domestic. I widened my eyes at him.

'Holy fucking fuck. He just said the M word.' Cass sounded as shocked as I was.

'He did.'

'He sounds like he means it too.'

'I know,' I said.

"I'm glad to know that you intend to do the honorable thing here," my father was saying, as if I wasn't in the middle of a huge holy-fucking-shit situation.

Brock squeezed my hand. "I've not yet asked her to marry me, but I assure you that day will soon come and I'll do anything to protect her."

Ohmygod. Did Brock just offhandedly propose? *'What's happening?'* I asked my bestie. *'Do something now!'*

"How did the Akuma find you, sir?" Cass piped up, walking around from behind my dad's wheelchair and taking center stage. "And what makes you think they'll find Evie next?"

Thank fuck.

My blood pressure started to return to normal as my father took the bait.

"I don't know how they found me. They shouldn't have been able to. My kitsune power is gone. Nothing but faint remnants of it linger, not enough for them to track me with it. I managed to hide from them for many years— until a couple of weeks ago. And I know they're hunting my daughter, because the demons asked me about her."

Even though I understood that he'd stayed away to protect me, it still stung to know he was alive this whole time and didn't tell me. If the roles were reversed, I would have found a way to get a message to my daughter.

As if he read my thoughts, my father reached for my hand. Unshed tears swam in his eyes. "Every second of every day we've been apart, I've thought about you. I wanted to call you a million times just to tell you I was alive."

I swallowed hard. "Why didn't you?"

He sighed, frowning. "It's complicated, but basically I had an inside asset with the Akuma right after the car accident with your mother. An old friend, a warlock. He said the Akuma were watching you for any sign that you bore my gifts. He said that if they thought you had even one shred of magic or might be a threat, they would end your life."

I squeezed his hand, swallowing a thick lump of emotion. "I understand."

He wiped his eyes. "I also know that you're your mother's daughter, and that if you knew I was alive, you would have tried to find me. That would have led the Akuma right to us both, so I had to remain vigilant, carefully plotting my course of action all this time."

Haru and Reo entered the room then, harried as if they'd run. I nodded toward my dad. "Haru, Reo, my father has come," I explained.

They scuttled into the room—most unlike them—circled my father's wheelchair to face him, and bowed low, their arms rigid by their sides.

Okay. This was a side I'd never seen of the warrior brothers.

My father nodded graciously like he was some kind of king, and only then did my protectors rise.

"Welcome, Master," Haru added. "How may we assist you?"

I finally realized that, despite his paralysis, my father was dressed impeccably, his hair cut and combed with precision. He raised his head in a regal manner. "I am here to protect and train my daughter. She must close the gate to the underworld. Since my physical body is no longer up to the task, I will assist you in training her."

Haru bowed his head in acquiescence. "Of course. It will be our pleasure. We've already begun her training, as you requested, but she does have to complete three more shifts before she acquires all nine tails."

"Because of the baby?" he guessed, and they nodded. "We have much to do in little time," my father continued. "The Akuma's most recent attack on me has left me weaker than I'd like. I need to rest before I begin Evie's training."

"You are welcome in our home, as is your ... attendant?" Brock cocked a questioning brow at the woman behind my father.

"Yes, this is Cho. She is both my nurse and a witch. Cho has helped hide me from the Akuma all these years. If you have space for both of us, I'd be grateful for your hospitality, though we will need two rooms," he added timidly.

"Welcome, Cho," Brock said. "We have enough room for both of you, and would be honored to have you in our home."

My father raised one eyebrow, like maybe he hadn't realized we lived together in sin until this very moment.

Kill me now.

"Thank you. I'm quite tired from the journey," my father finally said diplomatically.

Brock nodded. "Please follow my second-in-command, Ray. He'll lead you to your rooms."

Ray swept into the room as if by magic, though I knew Brock must have used his pack bond to call him. "If you'll follow me," Ray said, waiting for Cho to wheel my father around to leave.

"Wait," my father commanded, and looked my way,

reaching out to squeeze my hand. "I'm so pleased to see you again, kitten. We'll catch up more later." Emotion shone in his eyes as my throat went tight. And with that, Cho wheeled him from the room, leaving stunned silence in his wake.

I waited a full minute, long enough that I figured he couldn't hear me. "Wow. That was ... intense," I breathed.

Brock was grinning like a fool next to me; he totally liked seeing me squirm.

Cass barked out a laugh. "I've never seen you so nervous."

I released some of the tension I'd been holding. "I meet my dad for the first time, and in the first sixty seconds he's asking me why I'm not married. Who wouldn't be nervous?"

"You have to understand," Haru implored—I'd almost forgotten he'd entered the room. "The kitsune were treated like gods in our homeland and raised in a traditional manner. They were revered for their powers. Your father would have been raised like a prince, and later treated as a king once he took over the mantle of kitsune from his father. Your way of life might be a bit shocking to him until he gets used to it."

I was pretty sure Gran hadn't treated him like a king...

"Don't worry, he's just trying to protect his only daughter," Cass assured me.

I smiled. No matter how ludicrous the situation, he always had my back. "Thanks, Cass."

"You got it, babe. Now, I'm off to see T. I left her with Molly at the cabin and she's waiting for me."

I blew Cass a kiss, which made him waggle his shiny butt while he sauntered away.

"All right, guys," Brock said, looking from Reo to Haru. "My woman and I need some time alone."

Haru and Reo were suddenly all business. They stalked from the room in four seconds flat. When I turned back to face Brock, the room empty of people, he was already staring at me. "So what do you say? Will you marry me?"

Holy fuck.

My eyes bugged out of my head as my heart jackknifed in my chest. "No way! That's not fair. You can't do it like that after my dad pressured you."

Brock's eyes were like steel cutting into my soul. "Your father reminded me of what I've wanted to do for weeks."

I crossed my arms. "Okay. Then where's the ring?"

Brock grinned. "In my top drawer. I'll go get it."

I gulped, forgetting to breathe. "Brock Adams, you bought me an engagement ring?"

He just smiled wider, scooped me up into his arms, and stalked toward our bedroom. I was speechless and fucking terrified.

Marry my baby daddy?

Then he wouldn't be my baby daddy anymore, he'd be my *husband.*

We *just* moved in together.

'You're totally freaking out,' he said as he locked the door to our room and set me on the bed.

"Just a little," I squeaked.

Brock nodded. "That's okay. I know how you work." He pulled open the top drawer of his dresser, where he kept his underwear and socks, and started to rummage around.

I'm going to faint.

Finally, he pulled out a jewelry box, but instead of getting on one knee like I expected he would, he walked over to my side of the bed and set the black velvet box down on the side table. My heart was pounding so loudly, I could feel it vibrating in my ears.

Coming back over to where I sat on the bed, he knelt down in front of me. "I know you. You don't make hasty decisions. So I'm going to leave that ring right over there, and when you're ready to give me an answer, you can."

I hadn't realized I'd been holding my breath until it whooshed out of me. "Brock. I ... just don't want you to be doing this because I'm knocked up."

A sly grin washed across his face. "Evie Black, I've waited my whole life for a woman like you to come along. You're strong, confident, sexy as sin, and that night you chose me in the bar was the happiest night of my life."

A grin pulled at my lips. "Yeah, because you had a one night stand that blew your mind. What guy wouldn't be happy with that?"

Brock leaned forward and peppered my jawline with kisses, making heat pool between my legs. "The mind-blowing sex was amazing, obviously, but that night was the happiest of my life because my life intertwined with yours, forever."

Forever.

We were having a baby together and that meant *forever*.

I was trying to think of something intelligent or sweet to say when his hand dipped into the elastic waistband of my jeans, reaching low for the sweet spot.

Would sex with Brock for the rest of my life be the worst thing in the world? No, no it wouldn't.

I was dying to see what the ring looked like, but that would have to wait—pleasure surged through me like a wave, rippling up my center as I crashed my lips into his.

Shit! My dad was in the house!

But then Brock swept his free hand behind my head and pulled my mouth against his with an insistent passion I couldn't refuse. I wouldn't deny myself a quiet quickie with the man I was going to marry. I hadn't misbehaved this long to stop now...

I was going to marry this man. Holy. Fuck.

I might not have said yes yet, but my heart already knew what my decision would be.

I moaned at the thought of sharing a life with him, and Brock growled, pinning wild amber eyes on me.

In five seconds flat he was out of every stitch of clothing and kneeling before me. I couldn't help but ogle the alpha, and now that he was going to be all mine *forever*, I was allowed to, right? I trailed hungry eyes across every inch of him as he peeled my clothing off with a reverence that had my already-mushy heart melting.

When he spread my legs and positioned himself between them, I stilled in delicious anticipation. And when he trailed his lips from my mouth, to my neck ... across my breasts, and finally, down my stomach ... and further down, I closed my eyes and gave myself over to pleasure.

A lifetime of this? Sold. Sign me up.

3 FROM ONE KITSUNE TO ANOTHER

"FIRST THINGS FIRST, we must anchor your power to the land," my father said over his cup of hot tea.

The motherfucker had banged on our door at five am. *Five.*

If he wasn't my father, I'd have told him to stick it where the sun don't shine.

My eyes were barely open as I peered at the man who'd given me my kitsune gift. "Say what?" I mumbled, chugging my coffee like it was liquid gold.

My father wheeled closer to me while his nursemaid, the witch, leaned casually against the porch railing. "A kitsune and the earth are one," he said once he was next to me. "You must anchor your new powers to her so she can help you when it's time to close the gate."

I really wasn't in the mood for lessons. "Father..." I tried the word and it felt weird. "Dad ... listen, I'm pregnant and tired. Can this wait until I nap?"

The world had to be ending to get me up this early.

My dad shook his head. "No, it must be done with the sunrise. That's when the earth takes her first breath."

What. The. Fuck?

The nursemaid stepped forward. "When you bind your powers to the land, it will also protect you somewhat from the Akuma."

My father nodded in agreement.

Brock cleared his throat. "Anything that protects Evie is good with me, but what land? Her gran's land or mine?"

My father's gaze sharpened. "Both. Evie is the heir to both pieces of land, but your father took his part when he made a deal with the underworlders."

I gasped. "Dad!"

Brock frowned, shaking his head in denial. "No. We're protectors of the gate. Like Evie."

My father looked at Brock with regretful eyes. "That's what your father told you..."

Oh shit. Hadn't Gran's note said something about not trusting Brock's pack? Maybe she knew more than I realized. Maybe the land feud was more than I thought it was.

"No. He wouldn't." But as Brock stared out at the land, I knew he was thinking about how his dad had made a deal with the siren Calista, and how his brother had planned to follow through with the deal.

"He did," my dad said. "But that's okay, son. We're going to put things right today." My dad started to wheel his chair to the edge of the porch like he was going to leave.

"Wait, what? How?" Brock stood while I wondered how we were going to get my father's wheelchair down the porch steps. Then the nursemaid threw some sparkly dust at the wheels and he and his wheelchair floated, like Cass did.

Cool.

The nurse floated my dad down the steps before returning him to the ground. Magic seriously rocked.

After I quickly chugged the rest of my decaf coffee, Brock and I walked out onto the lawn and faced him. As an unusual hybrid, maybe I was more like a mutant than human. Maybe all I needed was a badass superhero costume. I pushed my fantasy away and forced myself not to let my amusement show on my face.

One look at the seriousness on my dad's face and all amusement ran away. Why did the Akuma and the underworlders keep screwing up my life?

"Energetically, we are going to give Evie power over the land again, just as I once had," Dad said. "But it will weaken your alpha power, son."

Brock and I collectively winced. This land was everything to him, to his pack. Without it, they didn't have a home, the pack didn't have a purpose. Territory was the single most important thing to a wolf.

Regardless, Brock nodded. "If it helps Evie..."

I looked at him with wide eyes. "Are you crazy? No. You'll weaken."

Brock shrugged, looking nonplussed. "If it helps you, I'll be fine."

Something dawned on me. "Wait. Brock made me a member of his pack—"

I couldn't even get the words out before my father leaned forward in his chair, rushing to spit his words out. "He what?"

I winced. "Was that bad?"

My father took a few steadying breaths. "Kitten, when your mom and I had you, we knew it was risky mixing bloodlines like that. For you to then go and have a child with a werewolf and to then become part of his pack..." He blew through his teeth. "It leaves a lot of unknown variables."

Brock looked at me nervously. "Well, it's too late to change any of it now."

Truth.

My father nodded. "You're the alpha. It may be that we transfer the land's power to Evie and you can still harness it through her, but I just don't know. What I do know is that the Akuma are looking for her and they will come. When they do, I want her at full power and on red alert."

We both nodded in resignation. My dad was kind of like a drill sergeant; he was definitely running this show while everyone else slept the day away.

"Take me to the gate," he said.

The terrain was rough across parts of the pack's land, and so my father's nursemaid Cho hovered his wheelchair across most of it. She set him down twenty feet away from the gate to the underworld, amid a cloud of colorful sprinkles of magic. The witch didn't even look tired from the effort, and I wondered how powerful she might be to have aligned with my father.

"It's so strange not to sense the gate anymore," my father said, staring ahead through the dim light of predawn.

Brock and I, who'd been staring in the direction of the gate, turned to face my dad. My father's stoic face was blanketed with grief, though I didn't think he realized it was so apparent. When I raised my brows in question, his shoulders slumped.

"Just being here reminds me of all I've lost. I miss the magic, but mostly I miss your mother ... and I regret all the time I missed out on with you."

Shit. As difficult as it'd been for me to grow up without parents, he'd had to watch his wife die. He'd had to live on knowing that I was still out there, just out of reach. Thanks to the fucking Akuma. My face hardened in resolve at the same time his did.

He waved a hand in dismissal. "Let's get to it. The sun will soon rise, and we have to be ready. Evie, my girl, you have to shift."

"I'm on it," I said, but then hesitated when I realized that meant I had to get naked in front of my dad unless I wanted to shred my clothes and then be naked after I shifted back to human. "Um," I started, but Brock was already leading me behind a copse of trees.

"You can shift here. I'll watch your back." His amber eyes sparkled with mischief.

"You just want to see me naked," I whispered, overly conscious that my dad was within hearing range if we didn't keep quiet.

Brock shrugged. "Hey, can you blame me? I'm smitten." He smiled, and my heart did a flip flop. He moved closer, all but pressing himself against me. His hands hovered around my body. "I can't help but want to be naked with you," he whispered, and I batted his grabby hands away.

I flicked my head in the direction of my father and his nurse, and he threw his head back and laughed. "You're all flustered. I like it."

I playfully shoved him away. "Move it. Let me get undressed already and on with it."

"As you wish," he said, but didn't give me much space, his gaze pinned on me, prepared not to miss a moment of my disrobing.

Thank God I wasn't shy—at least not normally. I placed my katana on the ground with care, then pulled off my shirt and bra, boots and pants, all the while holding Brock's gaze, enjoying the way it heated with every new inch of bare skin I exposed. Even with my little potbelly baby bump he thought I was sexy. Then I shot him a wicked grin that promised we'd take this up later, and closed my eyes.

Each time I shifted into my kitsune form, the pain receded a bit more, and I couldn't be more grateful. The first time, my shift had been pure agony. But now I pictured myself as a fox, envisioning my rust colored fur, lithe little body, and violet eyes, as I built the purple magic of my kitsune deep within my center. When it had expanded so that it felt like the size of a soccer ball, completely filling my chest, I pulsed the energy outward, toward the image of my kitsune shape I held in my mind's eye.

My magic tingled in a fast rush across my body, spreading from my center, across my limbs, and down my extremities. Then my form began to morph. My bones and cartilage cracked, my muscles snapped, my flesh stretched until ... I landed on four feet in the figure of a fox. I shook my head to free myself of whatever pain lingered from the shift and tried to look behind me.

Brock chuckled softly and spoke to me through our pack bond. *'You have seven tails. So crazy.'*

I felt a little bit crazy...

'Great. Just two more to go and we can shut this thing down,' I said.

'How does the gate look?' Brock asked me as I rounded from behind the copse of trees.

I sensed my dad's gaze on every one of my movements as I passed him and his witch to inspect the gate. *'It looks about the same. Maybe the crack has expanded a bit, but not enough to suggest we're in any deeper shit than we already were.'*

"Is my daughter communicating with you?" my dad asked Brock.

"Yes, through our pack bond. She says the gate looks about the same as it did last time she inspected it."

"Excellent. That's the best we could hope for at this point." Dad wheeled his chair closer to me. "Evie, we need to perform the ritual now. The sun is about to break the horizon. The ritual needs to be in progress when the sun appears."

I nodded my little fox head and looked at him and Cho attentively.

The slim witch, who appeared to be of Japanese ancestry like my father, walked over to me and took a seat on the damp earth, pressing her palms flush against the ground on either side of her. "Please join me, Evie."

But when I started to move in her direction, I stilled mid-step, and my jaw dropped before I managed to snap it shut. A ... projection of my fox form was standing two feet from me, to the side of Cho.

'What the fuck. Brock, are you seeing this?'

'Whoa. I guess we just discovered your new power. That's pretty wild...'

'Uh, you can say that again. There's another one of me standing where I was planning on going!'

"Evie has developed the ability to project herself," my dad said, sounding pleased. "That will prove a useful power when dealing with the Akuma."

He was totally unfazed, while I couldn't stop staring at a projection of myself.

"And the sirens," Brock added, reminding all of us we had enough enemies that they could form a club.

'But I didn't mean to project myself. I have no control over it,' I fretted.

The last thing I needed was another power I couldn't control.

'Don't worry, Evie. It's probably like everything else. With practice you'll learn how to use this new power.'

'Right,' I said, and continued toward Cho ... and the other little rust-colored fox with seven tails and violet eyes. My body double was peering at me like she and I were separate instead of one and the same. What a mind trip!

I settled on the other side of Cho, shaking my seven tails once to get a feel for the new fit. The witch tilted her face toward me, but didn't remove her hands from the earth. "All you have to do is follow my lead," she said. "I'm going to connect the power of the earth that runs through this land to you. I'll be directing the energy of the earth to link with you, so when you feel her energy, open to it. Don't pull away. No matter what you do, make sure you don't do anything to reject the connection I'll be working on forming. You need to embrace her energy, allow it to weave together with yours. Any questions?"

A million or so. They didn't make manuals for this

kind of shit. But I shook my head anyway. If I'd learned anything since discovering I was a kitsune, it was that I just had to roll with things and hope for the best.

"Will it hurt the baby?" Brock asked, of course always thinking about the baby. I internally chastised myself for not doing so myself.

Cho shook her head. "Mother Earth nurtures and gives life. Her magic will do nothing but support the baby."

Relief flooded through me.

"Alright." Brock didn't sound as sure, but what choice did we have at this point but to trust?

"Okay," Cho said. "By binding your power to the earth closest to the gate, our hope is that you'll be able to influence the land that contains the gate, helping you seal it once you have your nine tails."

I nodded, my communication skills as a fox being limited and all.

With a final look to the east, Cho's mouth settled into a tight line of determination. "Let's begin." She closed her almond-shaped eyes and dug her fingers deep into the dirt.

I was ready to hang onto every word of her spell, wanting to learn more about the witch side of my magic, but when she began she spoke in Japanese. And though I'd studied some Japanese, I wasn't fluent enough in the language to follow the intricacies of the spell.

Before disappointment could set in, my fur stood on end as the air around us electrified. A breeze whipped up, rustling the leaves of the trees that surrounded us and making the long grasses around us sway.

Whoa.

Cho's chanting increased in volume and intensity, speeding up until her words merged into what seemed like a single melody. The magical breeze circled the area around the gate, settling above us like a tornado.

I tilted my gaze upward, staring warily at the visible cloud of violet magic funneling above us, while Brock edged carefully around the area so as to be closer to me.

Then a bright purple glow began to seep up from the ground, dividing my attention. It was faint at first, but quite rapidly it thickened until it all but concealed anything behind it. My paws began to tingle as magic moved from the earth into me.

I shifted on my feet, resisting the urge to fight off the tangible magic pressing in on me. My fur whipped in every direction as the magic from above thickened, congealing into a fog that precisely matched the one rising from below.

Heavy, as if it were solid, the violet mist pressed on me from all sides, making me feel caught without escape. But Cho told me not to fight it, not to resist, so I clamped down on my instincts to fight, or at least to get out of the fog's way. Brock, Dad, and Cho were no longer visible, hidden behind the wall of purple that separated me from them. Though I couldn't see them, I could still sense Brock. Our bond to each other buzzed happily in my heart, reassuring me things would be fine. I could do this, though I felt like climbing out of my skin.

The purple mist grew thick enough that it transformed into a glow, settling across my fur like a neon coating. Cho's chanting rose to the next level. She was practically singing now. Her melody vibrated beneath my skin as the power continued to build, pressing in on me.

When what felt like electricity rose through the ground beneath my paws to vibrate through my legs, torso, and finally traveling into my head, Cho's spell reached its crescendo ... and the purple mist that surrounded me in every direction imploded like the collapse of a nuclear blast. The violet power sucked inward, consuming me entirely, before it blasted outward in a rushing wave that pulsed across all of the pack's land, leaving behind a clear sky, shot through with the first rays of the morning's sun as it peeked above the horizon.

My heart was beating a mile a minute, my flesh feeling like tiny ants were crawling all over it. I was panting like I'd just sprinted. I could almost feel the blades of grass moving in the wind, the roots of the trees that reached deep into the earth, as if all of nature were an extension of me. Was I now tied to the land's power?

Immediately, I searched out Brock. The beaming smile on his face suggested everything had gone well. I turned to Cho, who looked as pleased as my father.

'You all right, Eve?' Brock asked.

I nodded, working to release the tension from my body. *'I'm fine. That was just weird as fuck.'*

'It looked weird as fuck too. At least now there's only one of you again.'

I snapped my attention around our circle. He was right. There was no duplicate of me. That was a relief. I had enough to deal with without mirrors of myself running around—though if I learned to master the skill it could become a really cool party trick.

"That was excellent, Evie," my dad said. "The spell appears to have been a complete success."

"Absolutely," Cho added. "Everything went as well as

we could have hoped. Evie's powers are fully linked into those of the land now, I can feel it. With a bit of luck, the earth's power will give her the advantage she needs to seal the gate to the underworld, once and for all."

Sounded like a damn fine plan to me. Especially the luck part. I welcomed all the luck we could get.

'Ask them if I can change back to human?' I projected to Brock. When I got the okay, I trotted over to the trees where I'd left my clothes and made quick work of returning to my human body. I had questions to ask. With my katana back in hand, I moved over to the others.

"I don't really feel any different than I did before," I announced. Other than maybe feeling like I could sense the energy of nature around us, but that could be my mind playing tricks on me or some kind of remnant of the spell.

"That's okay," Cho said. "It definitely worked."

"Great. Now what?"

"Now we start your training," my dad said.

"I've already been training." I didn't want him to think I'd been sitting around doing nothing with Haru and Reo.

"Not the way I have in mind. The survival of all of humanity rests on your shoulders. We have to step things up."

I barely managed to keep from rolling my eyes. Step things up? How could things possibly get any more intense than they'd been over the last few weeks? It was barely 6 AM or something. The only thing I wanted to step up was my napping game.

As if I'd jinxed myself, I narrowed my eyes at the location of the gate, which I could no longer see now that I was back to being human, or as close to it as I got as a hybrid kitsune-witch. But I could sure as shit see the putrid-looking black-green fog seeping from what appeared to be a random spot in the forest, but had to be the gate.

"Uh, what the hell is that?" I asked, pointing.

As one, Brock, Dad, and Cho swiveled to look.

"Shit," Brock said. "That can't be good."

So he saw it too.

"It isn't," Dad said. "Cho, I thought everything had gone to plan?"

"It did," she said. "But maybe the force of joining Evie's power to the earth shook up the gate. Her power is substantial. It might have been enough to upset things inside the gate, especially if it's cracked open."

Well, that would have been a good point to bring up —*before* we bound my power to the land's and unleashed the nasty-looking green misty shit.

"We have to get inside. Now," my dad said. "It's moving fast, and if it touches us..."

"What happens if it touches us?" Brock asked, urgency vibrating through his words.

"I'm not exactly sure, but whatever it will do, it's the energy of the underworld, so it can't be good."

My father was right. The sinister looking mist could be poison for all we knew.

I gulped. "We have to stop it, then." What if it hurt someone?

"I don't know how to stop it, and unless you do, we should steer clear of something we don't understand. You're our only chance at stopping all of this chaos. We need to keep you and my unborn grandchild out of harm's way."

Brock's hand settled on the small of my back and he urged me forward. "Come on, Evie. We'll figure it out. Once you and the baby are safe."

Cho was already dusting her hands of dirt and flinging them in Dad's direction to hover his wheelchair. This witch was definitely powerful. The binding spell had been strong, and yet she looked as bright and eager as before, and it was still butt early in the morning.

I gave the green fog a wary look, hesitant to leave when there might be something I could do to stop it, though I'd probably have to be in kitsune form again so I could see where it was coming through the gate. I couldn't risk another shift so soon, not with the danger that might pose to the baby. Besides, the fog seemed to be rolling away from Brock's house and Gran's cottage, so we had time to think.

"Let's go," Brock urged again, and when he took off at a run behind Cho and my dad, I followed.

Seconds later, Brock was in my head, only this time his message was directed to the entire pack. *'We've got a problem. A green fog is seeping out of the gate. We don't know what it does, but it's gotta be bad news. Do* not *touch it. No contact. Get inside your homes and stay there. If you're out and can't get back home in time, stay in your cars or a locked building, all windows shut. I'll update again once we know more.'*

The day was barely starting, and already it'd gone to shit...

4 SHIT'S ABOUT TO GO DOWN

"BLACKISH GREEN, you're sure it was a blackish green fog?" Cass was pacing Brock's living room.

When I'd mind-messaged him about what happened, telling him to stay inside, he'd come right over. Tianna had sensed my merging with the land all the way over at his loft in town, and they'd already been on their way to see what the magical disturbance was about. Molly, Reo, and Haru were locked tight in Gran's cabin awaiting further instructions.

"It was mostly green," I told Cass.

"But it was also blackish." Brock trailed off in thought, rubbing his stubble.

My father was watching my bestie with one raised eyebrow. "Do you know what it is?"

Cass grumbled. "Well, I sure as hell hope not. The only fog demon I know of is from childhood stories, and if that's what we're dealing with, then this is a huge problem. *Huge*."

I swallowed hard. "Fog demon?"

Cass rubbed his little pot belly. "If it's a fog demon, the entire town could be in trouble."

My eyes widened. "The entire town?"

He nodded. "If what you saw is what I think it is, then things in Eugene are about to go south, and quickly."

My heart jackknifed in my chest. "How? Should we warn the townspeople? What do we do?"

Cass placed his little palms out in an effort to calm me. "No sense in causing panic. Besides, warning humans about a demon fog that makes them turn into raging murderers will only cause mayhem."

Raging murderers. He said *raging murderers.*

"What should we do?" Brock growled, moving to my side.

Cass sighed. "We call Detective Swanson and tell him what's going on, and we watch the news. If crime spikes, then we have a fog demon on our hands."

Oh God. Just what we needed. I was so close to sealing that gate! I only needed two more tails and then this would all be over with.

"And if it is a fog demon, how do we vanquish it?" my father asked.

"I have no idea. In the children's story I grew up hearing, the hero used a ten witch pentacle to kill it. Or something like that."

Both Tianna and Cho made a slight strangling noise in their throats.

"A ten witch pentacle?" Tianna asked in an agitated voice.

Cass nodded. "Purely fairy tale, I'm sure."

Cho and Tianna shared a dark look.

"Oh no. What is it?" I asked.

Tianna couldn't seem to find her words, so Cho spoke for her: "Only the darkest creatures of the underworld need to be taken down by a ten witch pentacle. It's a spell of near impossibility, and that's assuming you have the ten powerful witches you need to recite it while joined in a power circle."

"Ten!" I shouted.

Ten witches were hard enough to find, but ten *powerful* witches? We had two in this room—I was still riding with training wheels—and Willemena, if we could get her. *Three.* We had fucking three.

"Let's just hope it's not a fog demon," Cass said, shuffling his feet nervously.

The way my shit show of a life had been going lately, I'd bet my life it was exactly that.

"I'll call Detective Swanson and give him a heads-up," I grumbled, and shuffled to the back room that Brock and I shared.

The king-sized bed looked so comfortable. It was calling my name for a long nap. When I reached the side table to grab my cell, I noticed the unopened engagement ring box. I really wanted to open it because I knew it would be perfect, something amazing that Brock picked out with me in mind ... but now wasn't the time. We had a crisis on our hands, and I wanted that moment to be special.

Bypassing the ring box, I put in a call to the detective that Molly, Cass, and I had worked with on the siren case —before she escaped—and waited for him to pick up.

"This is Detective Swanson..."

"Hey, it's Evie Black. The bounty hunter."

He sighed. "Tell me the sirens aren't back."

I chuckled nervously. "They're not." The sirens had slipped out of police custody and I was the last one to see them. I'm sure Swanson didn't think too kindly of me.

"This is a different ... possible threat," I hedged.

I could sense him clenching over the phone. "I'm listening." Wariness dripped from each word.

"Well, my bounty hunting partner is from the under-world, and so his knowledge of underworld creatures is a bit better than mine, even though he was raised in Phil-adelphia, so it's really children's stories that he—"

"Ms. Black, I've got three open investigations. Can you speed this up?"

I took in a deep breath. "It's quite possible that a greenish black fog demon is rolling into town and it could make people a bit more murderous than usual."

Silence.

"Fog demon?" he finally asked, not bothering to hide his incredulity.

"Yeah, so ... it looks like fog but it's really ... bad. It influences people. Just let me know if you get a bunch of calls tonight. Like way more than normal."

He sighed. "And then you can come take care of it?"

I rubbed the back of my neck. "It's a bit complicated."

"Well, work on it! We need a plan in place if this fog is what you say it is."

He was right, absolutely right, and I knew what I needed to do to have a contingency in place if a fog demon decided to ravage the town. The very thought of the destruction it might cause made me sick with nervousness.

"You're right," I said. "I'm on it. I've got a plan. Call me if things get crazy tonight."

"Okay. Thanks for giving me a heads-up, Black." And he hung up.

When I looked up, Brock was in the doorway. "How'd it go? Why do you look terrified?"

Shaking my head, I rose from the very soft, very tempting bed. "It went fine, but I need to contact the Black family witches." I sighed heavily in resignation.

Brock's eyebrows hit his hairline. "The ones who made fun of you for not having magic and had issues with your grandma?"

"The very ones." Those motherfuckers were the only witches in a one-hundred mile radius that could help us. The Black witch clan was a powerful bunch, and I wouldn't trust anyone else to help with such a dire situation as a fog demon, if that's what we were dealing with. I might not like them, but I wouldn't deny the Blacks knew what they were doing.

"Where do they live?" Brock asked.

I sighed as the reality of having to call on them sank in. "Cottage Grove. Just outside town."

Brock crossed the room quickly and pulled me into his arms. "Want me to go with Tianna and Cass? You don't even need to be involved."

I barked out in laughter. "An alpha werewolf, a demon imp, and a fae-witch hybrid? Johnny Black will shoot you on sight. No, it has to be me."

A frown pulled at his lips. His chest puffed out as he went further into protective alpha mode. "So they're dangerous? I'll bring the pack."

I waved him off. "Not to me. Last time I saw Johnny he was trying to give me a wedgie while repeatedly calling me a dud."

Brock held me tighter. "I should kick his ass."

Laughter peeled out of me. "Johnny Black is one of the most powerful warlocks in America. Gran told me to steer clear of him in a phone conversation right before she died. Said she suspected he was doing dark magic for money. Revenge spells, that sort of thing."

Brock whistled through his teeth. "And you want to ask for their help?"

I shrugged. "If the town goes to shit overnight, we'll have no choice."

"I've got an idea." Letting me go, he went into the closet and started to rummage around in a box. Finally he came out with a big, black, studded ... dog collar?

Brock chuckled. "It's a hazing thing we do to new wolves, but it might also let me go in as your pet."

I actually choked on my spit a little as I snort-gasped. "You think Johnny Black won't know you're a werewolf?"

He waved me away. "Of course he will, but I'm not letting you go see them alone, and if you say I'm your pet dog, then he won't have to puff his chest out and go all alpha."

I grinned. Brock would wear a dog collar just to protect me? "Alright. Worth a shot."

I mostly just wanted to see this.

Brock nodded. "Let's do this. I have a feeling that wasn't any normal fog."

I had the same feeling. I also felt I wasn't going to get a nap in today, and that pissed me right off.

5 FUCKING FAMILY

BROCK WAS IN WOLF FORM, black leather collar in place, as he sat in the passenger side of his truck. He was no longer letting me drive my Jeep, saying it was too unsafe for me and the baby. It had taken me the better part of an hour to convince Cass I didn't need him to go with me. If Johnny or mean old Aunt Bertie saw him, they'd shoot first and ask questions later.

The Blacks cared about three things: money, magic, and power. If you were a threat in any way, they wouldn't hesitate to incapacitate you. The Blacks' ranch was a sprawling fifty acres with half a dozen cabins dotted on it, much like Brock's land. There must have been a dozen of my aunts, uncles, and cousins living there by now. I just needed seven. Seven witches or warlocks to help with our ten-pointed pentacle spell in the event we had a fog demon wreaking havoc on our town.

I hated that I had to do this. Groveling to Johnny Black was up there on my list of things I never, *ever*, wanted to do. He'd been a mean asshole growing up, and I was so thankful Gran chose to live away from them and claim her own space. I couldn't imagine living a cabin away from those pricks.

Before I knew it, I was driving down the dirt road that led to the Black land. My gran didn't tell me the whole story, but there had been a big falling out when she married my grandpa and decided to move onto her own property and leave their family compound. Something about her taking her power with her when she left. It didn't sit well with the Blacks, and they never forgave her for it. Then, when I was born without magic, it just added fuel to the fire. But I hadn't actually been born without magic—something I needed to keep reminding myself.

We reached the end of the dirt road to discover it blocked by a huge, black, wrought-iron gate. Pulling Brock's truck up to the speaker box, I pushed the button.

"Who's there?" a deep male voice asked right away. *Johnny?*

"Evie Black." I tried to keep my voice calm and steady, but it shook a bit.

There was silence for what seemed like a full minute before a wave of power washed over me and the gates opened.

'What the hell was that?' Brock asked from the passenger seat.

I had no idea. A spell that revealed a person's intentions? A spell to break all illusions in case I was someone pretending to be Evie Black? I didn't know enough about magic yet to know what it was.

'Something powerful,' was all I said in the end as I drove the truck right up to Aunt Bertie's cabin and parked. I had no idea if this was where Johnny lived now,

but it was the biggest and grandest home of them all, so I was hedging my bets that he'd taken it over. Most witches, like Willemena, were solitary. Dealing with a coven like the Blacks was all the more nerve-racking because their power was amplified by each of its members.

Stepping out of the truck, I opened the door so Brock could hop down. He was a huge gray wolf and there was no way in hell Johnny was going to believe he was my pet dog, but it was worth a try.

Walking to the giant double doors, I was about to knock when they opened a few inches from my raised fist. The smell of freshly burned sage spilled out and Johnny's green-eyed gaze fell on me, and then on Brock.

He spoke in firm tones: "You are welcome, but the werewolf has to stay in the car."

I put a hand on my hip. "This big ol' dog? He's harmless. Oh, and it's good to see you too. Is Aunt Bertie around?" I asked casually, eyeing the foyer behind him.

He raised one eyebrow, scanning me and stopping on my belly.

"You're pregnant with a werewolf's baby? Is it his?" He pointed to Brock.

Leave it to Johnny to figure shit out right away.

"Yeah, it is." I changed the subject: "Did you know my gran died?" There was no way Brock was letting me in the house alone.

Johnny's thick black eyebrows knotted. "Yeah, I did. Sorry to hear it."

"Well, are you letting her in or not? These cookies won't ice themselves!" Aunt Bertie hollered from the kitchen.

Johnny rolled his eyes. "I wish she would just die already," he mumbled to me.

"I heard that! Remember, I know where you sleep," Aunt Bertie called out, and my lips pulled into a grin.

Oh, the dysfunctional Black family. How I sort of missed them.

"Come on in. I guess the wolf can too, if he's muzzled." Johnny's lips twitched a little at the word muzzle.

'Motherfucker,' Brock spoke into my mind.

'Wanna wait in the car?' I asked him.

'Not a chance in hell.' Brock stepped slowly toward Johnny, lowering his head a little. Reaching out, Johnny placed a hand on Brock's muzzle, and green magical bands wrapped around his snout, binding it closed.

I winced. *'Does it hurt?'*

'Only my ego.'

Bless this man. He loved me more than anyone I'd ever met. We both stepped into the house just as my phone beeped with a text. I checked it quickly, worried it was the detective or Cass.

Detective Swanson: *'Calls have quadrupled. Multiple murder suicides. Meet me at the station in an hour.'*

Fuck!

I relayed the information to Brock mentally as I tried to school my features. If the Blacks knew I was desperate, they would use that against me.

"Evie Black! My, my..." Aunt Bertie called as I walked into the kitchen. "Grab a piping bag if you're staying. You'll pay your dues."

Didn't I always... "Yes, auntie." I tried not to growl.

Johnny grinned at how quickly I caved into her.

Fucker.

"She's pregnant with the werewolf's baby. Probably needs an abortion spell," Johnny told his mother.

My eyes bugged, and a low growl rumbled in Brock's throat. Reaching out, I grabbed the skin on the back of Brock's head and yanked because I knew he was two seconds from jumping.

"Actually, we're very happy for the baby's arrival," I corrected Johnny with a warning tone.

Johnny shrugged, but Bertie had yet to look at me, working away at icing her cookies. "So, you don't invite me to my sister's funeral and now you've surely only come because you want something. If not an abortion, then what?"

I released Brock's head and started to pipe cookies, because this mad woman would chastise me if I didn't multitask. "Well..." Fuck these assholes, it was time to brag about what I was and how much magic I actually carried.

"I'm actually not a dud." I dropped the icing onto the cluttered counter and crossed my arms. "I'm a kitsune *and* a witch, and I guard the gate to the underworld, which is on my gran's land. Earlier today, a fog demon broke through, and now it's affecting the town. I have three witches already, but I need seven more for a ten-point pentacle spell to vanquish the fog."

Silence.

Bertie had stopped icing, and even Johnny leaned forward from where he was perched against the island in the middle of the kitchen.

"Kitsune..." Bertie was staring off into space. "But you've also got the Black family magic?" She grinned.

I nodded. "And my mother's grimoire. I'm not that great yet, but yeah."

Bertie opened her arms and moved toward me. "I knew your granny's magic didn't die with your mother." She pulled me into a hug as my brow creased in confusion.

Being helpful for once, Johnny explained: "When Aunt Belinda left, she pulled her magic from the Black Coven. It was still there, but weak. When your mom died, it got weaker, then a couple of months ago it nearly completely died out with Belinda's passing. But only for a few days, because then it flared to life stronger than ever."

My jaw popped open. It was only a couple days after Gran's funeral that I got my katana and my witch magic awoke. That's what they felt flare to life. Me. I got Gran's magic.

Bertie pulled back and rubbed my belly. "And this little baby Black is going to be powerful too. I can feel it."

It took everything in me not to push her away. The Blacks were magic elitists, always had been. Now that they knew I had power, they would be after some of it for sure.

"So you'll help me?" Damn, I didn't even have to offer to pay them or anything.

Bertie pulled back and nodded happily, almost looking like an innocent old lady for a few seconds. "Of course dear ... under a few conditions."

Brock growled low in his throat, and Johnny took a step closer to my alpha. I stepped away from my aunt and closer to Brock. "What kind of conditions?"

I should have known. Money, power, and magic. That's all the Blacks cared about.

"All I ask is that you and the baby come around more.

Once a week to play with your cousins." Her voice was sweet, but I knew there was an underlying motive. There was *always* an underlying motive with the Blacks.

Johnny nodded. "I have a wife and two kids now. My youngest is three months old."

'This is a trap. What's the bigger motive?' Brock rumbled.

"Why?" I asked aloud, because I definitely agreed with Brock. "You don't want to get to know me and my baby. Does our being on the land make you more powerful or something?"

That had to be it.

Bertie bared her teeth. "Oh, you always were a clever little girl. Yes. Something like that. You being here makes the clan more powerful. We have a business to run, you know."

I nodded. "I do know. I'm a bounty hunter now and I've heard all about your 'business.'" I did air quotes for good measure, and Aunt Bertie narrowed her steely eyes. "Don't you sass me, child. Do you want our help or not?"

Dammit, I did. The town was on a murderous rampage, and I needed the Blacks to stop it. "I do, but I won't ever bring my baby around you. *Ever.* If you can settle for me coming by for an hour every two weeks, then you have a deal."

Bertie scowled, crossing her arms, but Johnny stepped forward and extended his hand. "Deal. Good to have you back, cuz." He winked.

'These guys are a real piece of work,' Brock commented.

'You have no idea.' Regardless, I shook on it. Last I'd heard, Johnny was the coven leader now that Auntie Bertie had stepped down, and so his word was law with the clan even if his mother didn't agree.

"Stay for a cookie?" Auntie Bertie asked.

"Nope. Round up the coven and meet me at the Eugene County Sheriff's office. We've got a fog demon to vanquish." I turned on my heel and stalked toward the door.

Some family members were impossible to get rid of...

6 FOGGY APOCALYPSE

AFTER OUR TUMULTUOUS HISTORY, I'd imagined I'd encounter resistance in getting enough of the Black Clan members to agree to join my cause, but even before Brock and I left Cottage Grove, Johnny had chosen the seven of them who would help us defeat the fog demon. Apparently Gran hadn't been exaggerating when she'd said Johnny was a head honcho warlock now. Even Aunt Bertie hopped to when Johnny told her to, though she did plenty of eye narrowing and flinging her hands about. She even threatened to shrivel up his manhood if he continued ordering her around.

Brock shifted from werewolf to human as soon as I drove us down the long drive away from Johnny and Aunt Bertie's home, passing the many cottages that spread across the Black family land. He shook his head, rubbing his hands across his face. "I couldn't stand that binding for another second longer. It was driving me crazy."

"It didn't hurt though, right?" I glanced his way. "Holy shit, Brock, you're naked."

He grinned, mischief lighting up his honey-colored eyes. "Glad you noticed." He didn't bother to cover up any of his, hmm, manly bits for a few minutes. He was all smooth muscles and lean planes, and I was half tempted to pull the truck over to explore them.

"Eyes on the road, love," he said, pleasure at my reaction evident.

Oh right. The road. I yanked my focus back to the front.

"So," I started, trying to return my mind to our next move while Brock grabbed his clothes from the seat behind him and started putting them on. "Johnny chose the most powerful witches to join us, so that's good. At least based on what Gran told me."

They were going to be about ten or twenty minutes behind us. They were still assembling the crew when we left.

"Tell me about them," Brock said while zipping up his jeans.

"Well, Johnny knows his stuff, or he wouldn't be in charge of the Black Clan, but as you see, he's a prick."

"That fact didn't escape me."

"Auntie Bertie holds her own. She was the head of the clan before Johnny came of age and came into the bulk of his power. I suspect she could probably still give him a run for the position if she were so inclined."

"And why isn't she? She seems to have enough grit to take him on."

I shrugged. "Gran never really told me, but I expect Auntie Bertie just got tired of it. She complains a whole lot, as you saw, but she probably enjoys her semi-retirement. It's a lot of work to run a clan of witches and warlocks like the Blacks. Not a one of them seems to do anything without griping first."

"I noticed. Makes me glad the wolves are more easygoing."

"Totally. I'm grateful for that too. I couldn't imagine living on the Black land with all of them." I shivered. "Or raising a baby among them. It will be challenging enough raising a kitsune-witch-werewolf baby without having all of them around, breathing down my neck."

"I'm glad you told Bertie you wouldn't bring the baby by," Brock said.

I glanced at him. "I didn't figure it'd fly with you, and there's no way in hell I'll let our baby be a part of anything they're up to."

"Not a chance."

"Yeah, the Blacks are dangerous. The less we see of them, the better. If Johnny really is dealing in dark magic, then it's definitely bad." I tightened my hold on the steering wheel. "The other five witches Johnny said were coming are my cousins. Gran was one of five siblings, and they all had lots of kids. I haven't seen my cousins for years, but they'll all be able to do what we need them to. Even when I left Eugene when I was sixteen, they were already powerful. I'm sure they're more so now that they've been training with the clan."

"Have you gotten word about Willemena yet?" Brock asked.

I shook my head, flicking a quick peek at the dark screen on my phone. "Cass said he'd text as soon as Tianna had news. If Willemena can't make it, then I'll have to ask Johnny to bring an extra witch, though I'd rather have Willemena. Gran trusted her, and she's played straight with us so far."

Brock nodded, sharp eyes peering out the windshield ahead of us. "Willemena seems to know what she's doing. I hope she can make it too."

"Any news from Ray?" I asked. Brock had left his second in charge while he was away with me.

"Not since we first arrived at Cottage Grove. A few of my wolves couldn't get home in time, but they're locked in their offices, windows shut, vents blocked, waiting for instruction. We've got to get this dealt with soon. If a single one of my wolves gets infected, I don't know what it would do to the rest of the pack."

I gasped. "I didn't think of that. The entire pack is linked!"

"Including you and the baby."

"Do you think the effects of the fog could travel along the pack link?" Dread weighed heavily in my gut.

"I don't know, Evie, I really don't. When something bad happens to any of us, we can all feel it. When Nathan died, it hit every one of the wolves really hard. I think it's possible that if the fog takes hold of one of us, it could influence the rest of us. I hope it's not the case, but we've never dealt with one of these monsters before."

I was busy considering how bad this shit show would really go when I noticed something up ahead on the road. I squinted, trying to make it out. "Is that ... fog?"

A blackish green-tinged mist rolled across the road. Bile rose up my throat at the sight of it.

Brock clenched his jaw. "Fuck! It sure is. There was no fog on this road when we first drove through. It's spreading fast." He clenched his hands into fists and grunted in frustration. "I don't know how to fight fog! Give me something I can hit or sink my teeth into, not this crap." He gestured wildly up ahead of us.

Poor Brock. He was used to being in charge and in control. Since I'd arrived in his life, very little had been within his control.

"We're going to have to drive right through it," I said while Brock turned off the air conditioning, double-checked that the windows were fully closed, and grabbed two gas masks from the back seat, where we'd stashed them earlier. I'd learned today that Brock owned a dozen gas masks. When I'd asked him why, he'd just said he liked to be prepared for anything. Right then, I was mighty glad he was obsessed with protecting his pack.

While I kept driving, he strapped the mask on me before putting on his own. We had no idea if you had to breath the fog in to be affected or if it could just touch your skin, but this was the only road to the sheriff's office and we couldn't wait if it was spreading this fast. Yeah, it was like the apocalypse in Eugene, Oregon, and we didn't have a second to spare. It was only going to get worse if I didn't find a way to seal the gate before that siren bitch Calista and her sisters could get back out to create more havoc.

The fog thickened ahead of us until it fully concealed the rest of the road behind it. I was forced to slow down. "Dammit! If we had all ten witches assembled right now, we could take it down."

Brock's truck crawled through the haze of blackish-green.

"Did it take over the whole town while we were gone?" Brock asked. Through the mask, he sounded a bit like a sexy Darth Vader, though his question sent ice water through my veins.

"I sincerely fucking hope not." But as I drove the truck through the fog, with no end in sight, panic started to thump in my chest. "Send Johnny a text to warn the Blacks behind us."

Brock fiddled with my phone and then set it down, watching the road ahead keenly. He didn't speak for a moment, and I wondered if he was checking in with his second-in-command via their telepathic pack link.

"Oh no," he finally said.

"What?" I asked right away, keeping my attention fixed on the road ahead of me. Visibility was limited to like five feet in front of us. It was going to take us forever to get to the sheriff's office like this, and the Blacks wouldn't be able to get there any faster, and they were still probably ten minutes behind us even though I'd told Johnny they had to hurry. Though I didn't think they had gas masks, they were powerful enough to magically protect themselves from the effects of inhaling the fog.

"Ray says the fog has completely overtaken pack land. He's locked up in our house, so he can't tell if the fog rolled back in from town to our property, or if more of the fog is seeping out of the gate. Could there be more than one fog demon? Or could one fog demon take over a whole damn town?"

"Dammit, I don't know! Cass would though." But I couldn't exactly call Cass with a gas mask strapped to my face. But if he was close enough...

'Cass!' I called out across our link, hoping I was within range. We'd never been able to figure out exactly how far our telepathic capabilities stretched. *'Can you hear me, Cass?'*

'Barely, but yeah, I can hear you. Shit's gone to hell faster than we thought. It's chaos over here.' His voice was muffled inside my head but it was there.

'Where's here?'

'T and I are holed up in my loft, but we're going to leave soon to meet you at the sheriff's. It's all over the news. People are going nuts out there. It's really bad.'

'Yeah, Ray says the fog has completely overtaken pack land, which means Gran's cabin must be in it too.' I worried at my lip. Molly was in the cabin with Haru and Reo, and my dad was at Brock's house. *'We're on our way to the sheriff's. We saw my cousin Johnny, and he's agreed to send seven witches from the Black clan. Did Tianna get a hold of Willemena?'*

'Yeah, apparently the cranky old witch had a premonition about her being needed. She was already on her way. She'll meet us at the station in twenty.'

'That's good news. We need all the power on our side we can get.' I sighed in relief. *'We might be late at this rate, but we're making our way straight to the station. Meet you there.'*

'You got it, my girl.'

'And, Cass?' I said.

'Yeah?'

'Be careful.'

I didn't want to think about anything happening to my demon imp bestie. Life had changed so much over the last several months as to become nearly unrecognizable; Cass was the one constant fixture in my life I could always count on, and I wanted to keep it that way.

'Don't worry about me,' Cass said. *'My badass T has some*

kind of spell that keeps the fog from touching us. You watch your back till I'm with you to watch it for you.'

I smiled through our link, wondering if he could feel me, before disconnecting. "Willemena's coming," I said aloud to Brock, before finding it too difficult to communicate through the masks. I switched to our pack link. *'We need to stop this fog demon, stat.'*

'You can say that again.'

We continued to crawl along the road until my right eyelid twitched at the slow pace. I'd agreed to be at the station in an hour; at this rate, if felt like we'd be lucky if we made it before nightfall.

I handed my phone to Brock. *'Text Molly and Cho and tell them to meet us at the station. Tell Molly to wear the mask you left her, and to make sure to bring her apprentice badge.'*

'What about Haru and Reo?'

I hesitated. In reality, I wanted everyone I cared about to stay safe and put. But that wasn't an option. Still... *'I don't see what they can do to contain the fog. They should go protect my dad, especially since we'll need Cho for the fog.'*

Brock nodded and got to typing, and when we finally pulled up outside the station it seemed as if ten hours had passed, though it'd only been ninety minutes or so.

We were definitely late.

I cut the engine and peered at the barely-visible building. Immersed in the thick, putrid-looking fog, it was like a haunted house, not a police station. It perfectly matched the rest of the scene. The trashcans lining the street were upturned, parking meters were bent and knocked over, and cars had been abandoned with their doors hanging open and engines left running. And that was only as far as I could see in the fog.

'It looks like the set of a horror flick,' Brock said.

I nodded sadly. How had things gone so wrong so fast? And how was the responsibility of the entire town squarely on my shoulders? It felt like I was carrying around a refrigerator on my back, and all my body wanted was a nice, long nap ... monster free.

I needed to close that fucking gate, like yesterday.

Car alarms blared in the distance, making the uneasy stillness of the town seem all that much more wrong. There wasn't a person in sight.

'Is it safe to walk through as long as we're not breathing it, do you think?' I asked, wishing—not for the first time—that I'd had the chance to learn more about my witchy powers. If Tianna could make a bubble that kept out the air, I should be able to as well ... if I'd learned how.

'I have no idea...' Brock trailed off. *'You'd better double check with Cass.'*

But just as I reached out for Cass, a rap on my driver's side window about gave me a heart attack. I yelped and jumped half a foot off my seat, before seeing that Cass was hovering at my window, flapping his little wings to keep him aloft. The fucker was laughing at me as I attempted to gather the scraps of my dignity.

Tianna loomed behind him, but she wasn't laughing. The Amazonian fae-witch with the great hair was shooting looks in every direction, her magic crackling between the open palms of her hand. The fog didn't seem to touch them. They were surrounded in a thin clear bubble of clean air. She spoke to Cass in their transparent bubble, and he relayed to me. *'My sexy T says she's going to extend the bubble to surround the cab of the truck until you and Brock are inside. Got it?'*

I nodded first at him, then at her behind him. Her magic flared as she pushed the invisible force of her power outward to bolster and expand her clear bubble. The moment she nodded at me again, I popped open the driver's side door and Brock and I slid next to them, pulling off our gas masks but clutching them in our hands. There was no way I was leaving it behind in the car, not with the way our day had been going.

"Let's move," Tianna said in her best military commander impersonation. "Hostiles are everywhere."

"I don't see anyone," I stated while hustling along the sidewalk in front of the station.

"They're there, trust me."

As if I'd summoned them, a horde of people began filtering through the fog. On foot, there was no chance of confusing them for usual townies. Their dress was normal enough, but their faces were locked in menacing snarls, their gazes gleaming with a manic possession that didn't bode well for anyone. A low grumble followed them, like the theme song of hell.

"Oh. Fuck," I said, my step faltering.

Immediately, Brock's hand went to the small of my back, and he hurried me back into motion. We tore up the front steps of the police station and barreled through the double doors. The second we were through them, the officer who'd been stationed as lookout snapped a bar back between the two handles, barring the door shut. With a tight mouth, he peered out the tempered glass panels, watching the street.

Molly materialized from the fog then and sprinted toward the doors, gas mask firmly in place, a shotgun in either hand. She was also encased in a bubble and I guessed it was Cho's work. Damn I needed to work on my witchy powers!

"Open back up," I yelled, and the man did as I asked, letting her slip inside before closing it again. I added, "We're expecting three more parties."

The police officer looked between me and the fog-demon-possessed people following our trail toward the station. "I don't think they're going to be able to make it inside. I can't let the rest of them all in."

"We need them to stop this fog, and they're right behind us. They should be here any minute," I told the officer, thinking of the Blacks, Willemena, and Cho. "Do what you have to do, but we need them inside, and fast."

Prematurely balding, the officer scowled like I'd just told him to hop on one leg while doing the impossible, but when Detective Swanson rushed out from the back of the station to greet us, he nodded curtly. "I'll see what I can do," the officer on door duty said.

Brock clapped him on the shoulder while Tianna let the bubble protecting us dissolve. "See that you do more than that," Brock said. "If the people we're expecting don't get in, we can't stop the fog."

The officer gulped so that his Adam's apple bobbed, then nodded nervously, his eyes wide and worried as he took in three women who would've looked like sweet little old ladies if not for the murderous slant of their features. The women pounded on the tempered glass panels of the front doors, making the officer jump, and the rest of us hurry to the back, following Swanson.

Eugene, Oregon, was like a freaking zombie apocalypse.

7 TOO MANY WITCHES IN THE KITCHEN

LUCKILY, it didn't take long for our ragtag group to assemble. The Blacks and Willemena had arrived. Detective Swanson gave us the rundown: Chaos had descended upon Eugene, and it wasn't going to let up until we did something about it. The cops were at a loss. The human world was completely unprepared to deal with a fog demon.

The detective, who looked like he'd aged a decade since I last saw him, scanned the many supernatural creatures gathered in the conference room around him. Fine wrinkles lined his eyes and crinkled his forehead. "The latest is that one of my officers is holding his family hostage, at gunpoint. He was the first to be hit by the fog, so far as I can tell. By now, the only ones of us on the force who haven't been hit are inside this station."

I'd only seen him, the guy manning the door, and a receptionist. Unless they had someone hiding in a back room behind a closed door, that was what the police force of Eugene had been reduced to.

"What's your officer asking for in exchange for releasing his family?" Willemena asked in a strong voice. Despite the clusterfuck that pressed in on us on all sides, she was radiating a calm I envied. "If he's holding his family hostage, he must be asking for something."

"Or maybe not, given that we're dealing with a *fog demon*," Aunt Bertie snapped at Willemena. Since I'd introduced Bertie and Willemena, Bertie had been trying to assert herself as top dog.

Willemena tilted her head to one side, her long silver hair shifting gracefully, while she waited for Detective Swanson to answer. She didn't even direct a look at Bertie, which only made my great aunt growl softly and shake her tight gray curls.

Detective Swanson appeared lost for a moment, before rubbing his hand across a tired face. "He's asking for ten buckets of KFC, extra crispy, and biscuits and butter."

My mouth dropped open for a quick second. I definitely hadn't been expecting that. "I take it you're going to give it to him?"

"I don't see much of a point. Before this, it was three large pepperoni pizzas, with mushrooms and extra cheese. And before that it was lo mein and moo shu pork."

"What, is the fog giving him the munchies?" That was one of the weirdest things I'd heard lately.

"I have no idea. I'd hoped you would," Detective Swanson said.

I turned to Cass, who was sitting atop the conference table, shaking his head. "I've never heard about something like this before, but I do know there's only one way to fix it," he said. "And you're looking at it."

The detective studied our group once more, before

finally appearing to give up. He sank into one of the chairs around the table, slumping immediately. "What can I do to help? Gary is good people. He's been with the force for more than twenty years. He loves his wife and kids. Not so sure about the mother-in-law, but he'll never forgive himself if he hurts any of them."

"We'll take care of it," Willemena said as Aunt Bertie rushed to speak over her: "We're on the job."

Johnny stepped between them, crossing his arms and glaring at them both. Neither of the witches appeared cowed in the least. Finally, he sighed and asked, "Where's your officer's house?"

"Ten blocks from here, but it may as well be a hundred miles with how hard it will be to get there," Detective Swanson said. "The fog's everywhere now, and even with gas masks on we'll still run into all the people."

"There's nothing to help that now, Detective," Willemena said. "Go gather what stun guns and rubber bullets you have while we make a plan."

Detective Swanson heaved out of his chair, groaning and huffing all the way. The second he was in the hall, he hollered for the deputy manning the door, and Bertie turned on Willemena.

"Who made you grand witch of this temporary coven? I don't know who you think you are, but we're not gonna be taking orders from you. My son's in charge here. He's the leader of the Black Clan. He's gonna make the plan."

"Actually"—I stepped between them—"there's no time for a pissing contest. We have the ten witches we need for the ten-point pentagram spell. The sooner we deal with this fog demon, the sooner everyone will be safe, including the officer Gary and his family. Molly, Cass, and

I will keep you safe from zombie townies, while you put down this fog."

"I'm going with you," Brock said, ever the protective alpha and baby daddy.

"Of course," I replied, because we'd wasted enough time as it was. We needed to contain this before things could get any worse, or before Gary asked for Taco Bell or something.

I turned to face the witches who'd be responsible for doing the spell. "Willemena, Auntie Bertie, Johnny, Cho, Tianna, and the rest of you." I nodded toward my cousins, all five of whom wore similar expressions of distaste. "Where does this spell need to be done?"

All of them tried to answer at once, seeking to command the floor, and shouting voices rang out so loudly that I couldn't make sense of anything through the clamor. All except Cho. I moved toward her, singling her out. "Where do we need to go, Cho?" I asked. She was calm and had a look on her face that said she had an idea.

"At the point of concentration of the fog, the place it's doing the most damage."

"Like the officer's house?" Cass suggested as he fluttered over my shoulder.

Cho smiled. "Like the officer's house."

"Good," I agreed, turning to take in everyone in the room, a room that was feeling more crowded with each passing second. "I'd prefer to keep us all in one place anyway. Cass, Brock, Molly, and I will watch your backs while Cho coordinates the witchy troops." I half expected Cho to shy away from the role, but she only nodded firmly, garnering a snarl from Auntie Bertie, upturned noses from my female cousins, and a pout from Johnny. Willemena and Tianna were the only ones who didn't seem to care who took charge as long as shit got done.

"Molly, I take it you have extra ammo?" I asked my purple-haired apprentice.

"Does demon fog make people go ape-shit crazy? 'Course I have extra ammo." Her mouth was set in a grim line of determination.

"Only shoot if there's no other choice. Aim to disable, not hurt." I knew she'd need to be reined in a bit.

"Obvi," she said, and I resisted a smile.

"I'll be at your side," Cass said, patting his black leather Gucci fanny pack and his gun in turn.

"I wouldn't have it any other way," I told my bestie.

Brock sidled up behind me, wrapping a possessive arm around my waist. He wasn't leaving my side either, and his body language was broadcasting it to all the crazy witches and the warlock in the room.

Detective Swanson swept into the space then, out of breath and harried, but armed to the teeth. He had two pistols in holsters on his hips, with extra magazines of rubber bullets, and a shotgun leaning against either shoulder. His deputy was armed in the same way, a deep sadness tinting his gaze.

"Come on, everyone," the detective said. "I hope you have a fine plan in place. It's a war zone out there, and the town is taking new casualties with every passing minute. Follow me."

Brock, Cass, and I walked behind him, ignoring the way Bertie tried to jostle Willemena in the hallway. I rolled my eyes, but refused to discipline women who were both probably over a hundred years old. Since witches usually lived well over a century, it was hard to determine their age once they went gray.

The detective and deputy pressed their noses against the back, utilitarian double doors, peering through the glass windows. "All clear," said the detective, and the deputy repeated the call. Then they yanked down their gas masks, kicked open the doors, and bolted for two large vans with the Eugene Sheriff Department logo scrolled across it. Detective Swanson fiddled with a key fob, unlocking the back for us, as I sensed Tianna's air bubble settling around us.

The moment we were all encased in the bubble, we hauled ass, jumping into the back of the vans and pulling the doors shut behind us faster than I thought this motley crew of supes capable of. We were packed in like sardines, and two seconds later Detective Swanson launched the van forward in a squeal of tires. The deputy was right behind us with the other van.

It was time to kill a fog demon.

8 HORRORS OF THE UNDERWORLD

I PEERED around the back of the van, taking in the many sets of determined expressions. Even Bertie had put aside her displeasure in order to execute our strategy. It was a decent plan, despite the fact that so many things could go wrong. It was also our only plan.

"You're sure you can keep the air bubble around us while you do this?" I asked Tianna.

"Of course my girl can," Cass said right away, sitting on Tianna's lap in the back of our van.

Tianna smiled behind a wave of shiny, copper hair. "It won't be a problem unless the fog claims me, and it can't get to me in the bubble, so we're good."

"Now don't go boasting, girl," Aunt Bertie said. "Maintaining a spell of that level while also participating in a ten-point pentacle is no joking matter. Only a very powerful witch could do that and—"

"Your concern isn't necessary. I've got this," Tianna cut her off, and the air within the van crackled with an unseen power.

Bertie crossed her arms over her ample, sagging chest, making me glad for like the thousandth time since she'd arrived at the precinct that I didn't live in Cottage Grove with the rest of the crazy Blacks. She narrowed her steely, wrinkled eyes at Tianna. "I'll be watching you."

"And I you," Tianna shot back before pinning her attention on Cho.

Cho was somber, sitting on the edge of her seat. "We'll have to be fast out there. We—"

"You can't hurry good magic," Bertie interrupted.

Willemena huffed and flung her hands in the air. "Will you shut up, woman?"

"Hey! Don't talk to my mother that way," Johnny said. "Only I get to talk to her like that!"

Every Black in the vehicle voiced their complaints all at once.

At this rate we weren't even going to make it to the fog demon before everyone killed each other.

From the edge of his seat, Brock, with glowing yellow eyes that promised his wolf was close to the surface, growled so viciously that everyone shut up all at once. He held Bertie's eyes the longest. "There's only room for one alpha in this van, and that's me. Stop acting like children or my wolf is going to come out and do something about it."

Johnny gave Brock a murderous look, and just as I was about to intervene, the van slammed to a halt.

Brock pounded on the wall that separated us from Detective Swanson. His door opened and ten seconds later we were pouring from the back of the van, fully enclosed in Tianna's protective bubble. Molly and a few of my cousins jumped out of the other van, making their way over to us with the deputy right behind them, and slipped into Tianna's bubble.

The fog was thicker here even than it had been at the station. This was definitely ground zero, where the demon seemed to be concentrated. We needed to cut off the problem at the source, or lots more people would be dying—and soon. Our priority had to be getting rid of the damn demon fog once and for all.

"Detective," I called out, "I think you and your deputy should stay with us. The fog is out of control. If we can dispose of the fog demon, your officer and his family will be fine."

Detective Swanson took one look at how dark, thick, and menacing the fog that surrounded us was and nodded curtly. "I don't think we have a choice," he lamented. "Let's get this done."

After that was settled, I was pleased to see that everyone left the squabbles behind and executed their part in the plan with perfect focus and efficiency. Detective Swanson and his deputy planted themselves on the edge of what I assumed was Gary's lawn, gas masks firmly in place despite the fact that Tianna's bubble encompassed them too. The green fog was so thick here that it made it hard to see the bush a few feet in front of me. This was definitely where it was strongest.

Brock, Cass, Molly, and I created a loose square around the witches and warlock, protecting their backs. Nothing was more important now than dispatching this fog demon. My five female cousins, Paula, Melody, Caroline, Amy, and Samantha, spread across the well-kept lawn to mark the outer five points of the pentagram. The strongest of the witches and warlock positioned themselves to mark out the inner points of the pentagram. Cho, Willemena, Johnny, Tianna, and Aunt Bertie settled within an arm's length of my cousins, stances wide and firm.

"Ready?" Cho called out as the fog rolled against Tianna's clear bubble. As if the fog realized what was about to happen, it pressed against the bubble, appearing to try to crush it.

If Tianna hadn't been wearing her signature kickass confidence like an outfit, I might have been tempted to double check that the bubble would hold. But if Tianna was sure, then so was I.

"Here we go," Cho said, louder than before as the fog gathered power, pounding against the bubble, sounding a bit like the break of the ocean.

The petite woman flung her arms out to the side and started chanting in rapid-fire Japanese. Where had my dad found this witch? She definitely knew what she was doing.

After a minute of calling out the spell from memory, a line of searing white fire burst to life between Cho and Willemena on the inside, and between Paula and Melody on the outside, forming the start of a physical pentagram of fire along the ground. Johnny looked at the witch with a raised eyebrow, and I knew he was impressed.

Cho, Willemena, Paula, and Melody spit on the ground, contributing their physical energy to the spell and anchoring it. When each of them had also pulled out a few strands of hair and thrown them to the fire in an offering, Cho moved on to the next part.

The fog pounded harder against Tianna's bubble, shaking it, making it tremble like we were inside a layer of

Jell-O. Brock, Cass, Molly, and I watched the bubble warily, ready to intervene if something were to go wrong. It was our job to protect the others while they completed the anchoring of the spell, though the best we'd be able to do against the fog was have Cass and I hurl our magic at it. This fog demon was a fearsome adversary.

After another minute of Cho's chanting, white fire seared to life in another line, connecting Willemena to Tianna, and Melody to Caroline, completing the second line of the pentagram. Tianna and Caroline spit and tossed their hair, and Cho started chanting again, her arms still held aloft, facing out toward the encroaching fog.

When a third line blazed to life to connect Tianna to Johnny on the outside of the pentacle, and Caroline to Amy on the inside of it, the fog roared and thickened, coating Tianna's bubble so densely that it became impossible to see outside of it. I cast a wary glance at Detective Swanson and his deputy where they cowered along the inside edge of the bubble.

"Is that supposed to happen like that?" the deputy asked, backing away from the fog and closer to the center of the protective bubble, stopping short of interfering with the pentacle. None of us were going anywhere until the spell was completed at this rate.

"Of course it's supposed to happen like that," Cass answered reassuringly, but I knew my bestie. He was just trying to calm the guy; he didn't know shit about magic other than the few things he could do. Freaking out wouldn't help anyone, and with the way the deputy's entire face seemed to twitch, he was one more crazy experience away from losing it.

A shot rang out from the house then, immediately followed by screams. All of us protecting the witches and warlock swiveled in the direction of the house, though we could no longer make out its outlines.

"We have to help them," Detective Swanson said, but even he had to know we were doing all we could to help his officer. Once we destroyed the fog, its hold on the man would break.

Brock clapped a hand on the man's back. "You continue to protect the witches. I'll go try to see what's going on in the house. Hopefully it was just a warning shot."

"I'm already on it," Molly called out as she slinked through the bubble and away into the thick fog with her gas mask firmly in place.

My eyes widened. *What* did that crazy bitch just say? "Molly, I forbid it! Get back here."

"Shh, don't worry," she called back over her shoulder. "I'm just going to peek in a window. If anything makes a move for me, I'll blow its head off."

Oh God. My apprentice was a lunatic!

"Her balls are bigger than mine," Cass commented.

Molly was already gone, and Brock was left standing there like a fish out of water, looking between me and the direction of the officer's house, probably debating whether he should stay with me or go help Molly.

My apprentice had said she'd only take a look, and in the end Brock remained at my side, watching the fog pound against Tianna's bubble as if it realized what we were working to accomplish here.

The detective appeared somewhat mollified and returned his attention to the witches. All our hope was with the ten-pointed pentagram spell. I cautiously peered out beyond our bubble into the fog and any zombie humans that might emerge from it. I really didn't want to shoot anyone.

Cho was practically yelling to be heard above the enraged roar of the fog. The more of the spell she completed, the thicker it grew, and I suspected this was the fog demon calling on all its parts to concentrate its power in one place for a fight.

When a fourth line sparked to life in continuation of the pentacle, the fog screamed, making me flinch and cover my ears until the screeching cry abated. Bertie and Samantha spat on the ground and flung their hair into the fire amid worried glances at the bubble above us. It seemed impossible that something invisible could protect us against such a powerful force as the demon fog, but it held.

Cho shouted, flinging her hands in blazing gestures above her head. The fog, now a thick cloud of putrid black, pushed in on the bubble, squeezing and indenting it in places ... but Tianna's protection held.

Thirty seconds later, the fifth and final line of white fire raced across the grass to complete the pentagram, linking Aunt Bertie to Cho on the outside, and Sam to Paula on the inside of it. The pentagram was finally complete, and holy shit did it look awesome.

Every witch and the one warlock spat on the ground three times in quick succession and cast several more strands of hair into the blinding white of the line of fire. The light of magic consumed the hair offering, sputtering and arching ever higher.

The fog demon roared so loudly I thought my

eardrums would surely shatter. The detective and deputy shrank into a ball against the ground, taking cover.

Cass and Brock drew in a quick breath beside me, and I tilted my attention upward.

"Holy shit," Molly breathed, slipping back inside Tianna's bubble after her stakeout. She looked unharmed, and for that I was grateful. I agreed wholeheartedly with her expression.

Directly above Cho's head, pressed against the bubble, were three huge, bulging, grotesque eyeballs. Placed without apparent order amid the fog, the three eyes glared at Cho, and then at the rest of us. They were yellow around the edges, with large, black pupils of varying shapes and sizes. And they all promised death if the monster could break through Tianna's shield.

My breath caught in my chest; I reached for the hilt of my katana, though it wouldn't help me in this particular fight. One look at Tianna told me the witch was still confident her protective magic would hold, but also that maintaining it was straining her. Beads of sweat ran down the sides of her face. The demon fog was placing the entirety of its intent toward breaking her protection.

"How's the family?" I whispered to Molly, not taking my eyes from those of the fog demon.

"Scared, but alive. It was a warning shot. The cop seems to be warring with himself, fighting the demon's power over him."

That was a relief, and I could see it in the deputy's face.

The demon fog completed coalescing itself. From the dense black of its body, I guess, appeared a large, gaping maw. It roared again, this time rattling the fear loose from me as pointy, jagged teeth took form in its mouth, apparently out of nowhere.

Oh God.

Cho screamed out the rest of her spell, but I could no longer make out any of her melodic Japanese. My dad's witch was engaged in a battle of wills with a demon fog straight from the underworld, which meant it had arrived with all of its power undiluted. She shook from the power needed to maintain the spell.

The remaining witches and warlock began to show signs of their own strain as Cho's power linked to theirs through the spell. My cousins, the weakest among the bunch, though they were in no way weak compared to normal witches, began to quiver from the strain first. Willemena, Tianna, Johnny, and Bertie lasted the longest, until eventually they, along with Cho, began to tremble from the effort of trying to trap the demon fog and hopefully blast it out of existence.

When Paula and Amy began to convulse from the strain, Cho let out an almighty roar, filled with so much power it electrified the hairs across my arms, and Brock pressed himself against my back.

The demon fog produced hands out of the dense wall of black and began to pound against the bubble, which had started to shake alarmingly in a way it hadn't done before. It suddenly looked like the demon might break through.

Cho looked like she was fighting to keep her eyes from rolling back in her head.

"Fuck," I breathed in a terrified whisper. "It's not enough. We need more power."

"No, Evie, no way," Brock said.

"I have to," I said reluctantly, while bringing a protective hand across my belly. "If I don't add my power to theirs, our baby might not have a world to be born into. This fog spread to the entire town overnight. Imagine what it could do if left unchecked."

"I'll link my power to yours," Cass said. "That'll help."

I nodded and smiled sadly.

'Brock, can you lend me some of your power?' I didn't want to mention out loud that I wanted him to add his alpha power to the mix. That ability was secret.

'We don't know how much of it I have left after the earth binding ceremony,' he said. *'Whatever is mine is yours, but don't you dare let harm come to you or that baby of ours. Promise me you'll pull back if you feel it will injure either of you.'*

'Of course. I promise I won't let any harm come to our baby. Ever.'

The demon roared louder than I thought possible, threatening to crush the last speck of fight in any of us as I stepped forward, fists clenched.

Bring it, you fog demon motherfucker.

We were out of time. With one last glance at the three horrendous eyeballs and those gaping jaws wide enough to clamp the bubble in two, I ran for Cho. Brock and Cass were right behind me.

The white light connecting the ten sorcerers flickered, and I knew without a doubt that if I didn't help the spell would fail; Tianna's protective bubble would probably fall soon after, exposing us all to the fog demon.

I plastered my hand against Cho's back, clammy from the effort of sustaining the spell. Purple light shot from my palm and straight into her skin. Brock pressed his hand to my bare waist, and half a second later I felt Cass' stubby, four-fingered hand as well.

The white, blazing pentagram flared to life as magic coursed through me and into Cho. The flames marking out the five lines of the pentacle surged past their previous levels. I sensed Brock's magic running through me, the entirety of his pack's power behind him, and I knew that the earth binding spell hadn't weakened him at all due to our bond. If anything, it had strengthened him. I wasn't sure how, but that's how it felt.

Cho screamed as her body rocked from the increase in power streaming through her. A second later the eight other witches and the one warlock bellowed in joined pain.

When the pain of so much power became unbearable even to me, and I felt my own scream coming up my throat, Tianna's bubble collapsed.

In the exact same moment, the pentagram sucked the fog demon within its fiery light, trapping it within the five searing lines of magic.

The fog demon shrank to fit the size of the pentagram, becoming the size of a very enraged and dangerous bear.

The demon turned in a frantic circle, trying to escape the trap.

But it couldn't. It bellowed its defeat, bringing every single one of us, including the policemen, to our knees.

Still, we didn't break the link. Our power alone was containing one of the greatest threats to ever escape the underworld. Now that I was a part of this spell, I could feel the fog's sickly demonic magic pressing against the corners of my mind, fighting to get in.

My magic, and Cass' and Brock's, and that of every one

of his wolves, kept pulsing through me. We couldn't give up now. If we did, it'd all be over.

I grit my teeth against the demon's wrath and continued to stream my amassed power into Cho. The baby was still all right, proving that Aunt Bertie was correct. The little nugget was going to be crazy powerful. Now I just had to give it a decent world to live in.

I roared and powered on. The unified battle cries of our team echoed in my ears, blotting out the enraged bellow of the demon fog.

"Give me everything you've got on the count of three!" Cho screamed.

The group's faces set into grim lines of determination.

"One!" Cho roared, and I felt Brock and Cass pulse magic into my back.

"Two!" Cho grew louder, and the beast slammed so hard against the fire wall containing him that it flickered for a split second.

"Three!"

With that I pushed every ounce of magic I had within me.

"Die, motherfucker!" Cass shouted over my shoulder.

The fog demon gnashed its teeth and screeched a terrifying cry, pounding against the invisible force of the spell. Then the pentagram lit up like a Christmas tree. At the same time, the fog demon exploded into a ball of blinding light and dissolved into greenish, black ash, a small inoffensive-looking pile on Officer Gary's front lawn.

Cho and the rest of the witches fell backward from the burst of energy. Brock pulled me out of the way just in time.

We'd done it. We'd killed that bastard and saved the town.

I stood there for a moment just catching my breath.

Crotchety old Aunt Bertie looked at Tianna and Cho then, catching her breath. "If you ever need a coven, we would welcome you with open arms."

Clearly Auntie B was impressed with their power.

Johnny stayed silent.

Tianna nodded. "I prefer to work alone, but I wouldn't mind sharing a drink."

The detective stood, brushing off his pants. "A round of drinks for everyone. On me. After that crazy shit, we've sure as hell earned it."

I grinned. "Let's all meet at—"

My words were cut off by the sight of Molly aiming a shotgun at Cass' head.

I didn't think, I just burst forward like a fucking ninja and high-kicked the shotgun, knocking it out of her hands.

"What in the hell?" I shouted, rounding on my apprentice.

Oh. Fuck.

Her eyes were completely black.

"Cass, tell me this doesn't mean what I think it means," I groaned, staring at my not so sweet apprentice.

My bestie flew over my shoulder to take in the possessed version of Molly before us.

"Yep," he confirmed. "Some of the fog demon jumped into her before we killed it."

Molly lunged forward, hands out like she was going to strangle me. Brock gave her a quick knock to the temple with the butt of his handgun.

As he caught her limp body, he looked up at me. "Postpone the drinks. Meet on my land so we can sort Molly out."

Are you fucking kidding me?

Never a dull day in the life of a bounty hunter.

9 KILL IT WITH FIRE

MOLLY AWOKE in the truck halfway to Brock's and started cursing like a sailor, trying to head-butt Johnny and Willemena, who sat on either side of her. She was magically restrained but powerful, way too powerful for a human.

"This would never have happened if she weren't human," Willemena said.

"We can do an eviction spell," Johnny offered.

"And risk that demon tearing her apart on its way out? No way," Willemena said.

Tearing her apart? Oh my God. I couldn't handle this. Not Molly. Why was she always the one getting in harm's way?

I'd already called ahead and warned Haru and Reo what had happened. They were in some thruple relationship with Molly and I didn't want to blindside them by driving up with her in this condition. As Brock pulled onto his land, the two warriors were already outside in his front yard waiting for us, standing beside my father's wheelchair. Worry lined all of their faces.

"Those are her...?" Johnny had heard my conversation in the car that alluded to calling Molly's lovers.

"Boyfriends. Plural," Willemena said with surprising pride.

I grinned at the old broad. *Girl power.*

"Even the older dude in the wheelchair?" Johnny sounded completely mystified.

My grin fell. "Eww, no! That's my dad."

Before Johnny could retort, Brock threw the truck in park and jumped out, hurrying across the front of the truck to open my door.

Haru rushed over to us, looking more worried than I'd ever seen the stoic warrior. "Molly. Baby." He spoke with absolute adoration.

Molly's head tipped down so that she looked extra horror movie creepy. "I'm going to skin you all alive." Her voice sounded like wicked sandpaper.

"Oh God." Haru recoiled, stepping back a few paces and knocking into Reo. The brothers wore matching expressions of despair.

"Yeah, she's not exactly herself..."

Brock and Johnny hauled Molly out of the truck. Tianna pulled up behind us in her cherry red '67 Mustang Fastback, and she, Cass, and Cho got out and joined us.

"We killed that thing! How is this even a possibility?" I asked the surrounding group.

Cho rubbed her chin. "We did kill it, but a small part of its essence must have jumped into Molly. The fog demon is only alive now because of its host."

Host. What the fuck?

"Molly. Her name is Molly," I said.

Cho nodded, looking sad. "Right. Because Molly is human, it's able to control her, and she's too weak to evict it."

Oh Jesus. I felt sick.

"We can try to trap what remains of the fog demon and pull it out with a pendulum, similar to a house clearing spell," Johnny offered. "It's more gentle." We'd told the rest of the Blacks to head home. Johnny had agreed to stay on and help us figure this out. Maybe the Blacks weren't all bad after all.

"Hmm," Tianna mused. "Not sure it will be strong enough to pull out this level of demon, but it's worth a shot."

"Don't you fucking touch me!" Molly roared.

Oh God. Seeing her like this ... it killed me.

"Do it," I told them. I knew Molly would want to try anything possible to get this thing out of her.

Tianna and Johnny circled her while Brock stepped forward with Ray to grab one of her arms each. Brock had used his telepathic link with Ray, who'd appeared out of nowhere, to warn him of the situation. Willemena and Cho watched on, eyes astute, following every one of their moves, while Haru and Reo hovered around them, acting a bit like worried hens, something I'd never seen the warriors do.

"Shouldn't take long," Tianna told me. "We'll know right away if it's working."

"Shall I lead?" Johnny asked our fae-witch hybrid with only a quick glance at Cho and Willemena, who seemed content to take a back seat to the action.

Wow, Johnny asking permission for anything meant

Tianna had gained his respect. I was certain that didn't happen often, but Tianna was no ordinary witch. Neither were Willemena and Cho for that matter.

Tianna simply gave him a curt nod, while I silently thanked the universe that Aunt Bertie had decided to go home with the rest of the Blacks. If she were here, she wouldn't like Johnny being so deferential to another witch, and we all would have heard about it.

"Evie, take off her shoes," Johnny told me. I didn't question his command. I stepped forward, bending a little awkwardly over my baby bump, and wrestled with her bucking legs as she screamed and thrashed, mindful not to get kicked anywhere that could harm the baby. Finally I managed to press her bare foot on Brock's front lawn and step back.

My cousin clapped his hands together and sparks of white magic leapt from his palms. "I call on the cleansing energies of Mother Earth to assist in this clearing, to surround Molly with your protection..." A magical charge settled in the air, like an electrical storm brewing around us. I could feel a stirring in the earth, which was crazy, but at the same time made sense because I was now tied to the earth. My eyes flicked up to meet Brock's, and I knew he could feel it too, through our pack connection.

"Fuck off and die, witch boy!" Molly hissed.

A whimper caught in my throat. This so wasn't our Molly.

Johnny pulled a pendulum from his pocket and swung it before Molly. Her gaze fixated on it as he swung it left to right, left to right, over and again in a circle.

Tianna stepped forward, arcs of magic rolling off of her hands and winding around Molly's body. "I call on the energies of Mother Earth to sweep through Molly," she declared, calling the spell out in a strong, booming voice, "to disconnect all holds the demonic energy has on her, to disconnect any and all cords that bind them together. Remove any and all energies that do not serve her highest good, releasing her from their influence. Let all impurities be washed away. Only light remains."

For a second I thought it might work. Molly was watching the pendulum like a zombie, while Tianna's spell had encased her body in a cocoon of light. But then Molly tipped her head back and laughed. She full-on creepy laughed and my stomach sank. Disappointment rippled through our group.

"This won't work," Tianna said, huffing in frustration. "Molly needs to fight it herself. It's the only safe way."

"She's human. How the hell is she supposed to do that?" I clenched my fists, trying not to growl.

Molly thrashed in Brock and Ray's hold.

My father, who'd been silent this entire time, wheeled forward. "It's quite obvious."

I raised one eyebrow at the man. "Enlighten us."

My dad's gaze fell on Molly; her eyes blazed with hate as she stared him down. "Something similar happened in the village where I grew up. The only way the human was able to be saved was to remove her humanity."

We all stared at him, deadpan. He continued: "If we were to make her not human anymore, she'd have the strength to fight off the demon herself. In my village, a vampire turned the girl so she could resist the demonic possession, but in this case a werewolf would do." He smiled grimly.

Chills ran up the length of my spine. "You're not suggesting..."

"No way in hell," Brock snapped.

My father shrugged. "If Molly were changed into a werewolf, she would have the stamina and power to evict the demon herself. I'm sure of it."

Why couldn't I get a break? Just a little tiny, itty-bitty break without all hell breaking loose? Was it really that much to ask?

Cho threw her hat in the ring: "I agree."

"Unfortunately, so do I," Tianna said, holding Cass' hand and towering over him, in a cute way. "I've heard the same stories ... that in cases like these, if the human is turned they gain enough strength to fight the darkness naturally."

Haru swallowed hard and stepped closer to Molly. "She would approve. She's been talking about wanting to become a supernatural since the day we met her."

And I'd suggested it on the boat ride back from the selkie cave when she'd almost died. But still ... this was a huge decision.

My gaze flicked to Brock and he grimaced. "Even if the werewolf council were to approve it, she could die. You don't just bite a human and they turn into a werewolf an hour later, simple as that. Not everyone survives the change."

"Yeah, I remember, but Molly is strong." It wasn't too long ago that Nathan bit me and I was the one shifting into an animal. It was painful and foreign feeling, but I'd survived. Hell, I'd thrived—and so would Molly. She had the balls for it, that was for damn sure.

Brock let Molly go and Cho stepped in his place. He

grabbed my arm and pulled me aside. "Evie, do you understand what you're asking of me?"

I gulped. "Yes. I think this is the only way to save her, and time doesn't exactly seem to be on our side. Look at her."

Molly, sprawled out on the ground between Ray and Cho, looked feral, trying to kick out at Cho.

Brock gritted his teeth as Molly yanked against the grip Cho had on her ankle. My alpha looked tired. Hell, I was tired, but this needed our attention now.

"I'll call the council and ask," he finally said. "But be prepared. They might say no, and if that's the case ... I can't go against them or I'd be risking the whole pack. We need the council's sanction."

I nodded. "Just tell them what's going on and see what they say. That's all I ask."

Brock pulled me farther away from the group. He placed both hands on my shoulders and met my gaze. "Today was a big day—huge—and you haven't rested at all. Go lie down now. I'll get Molly as settled as she'll let us, and then call the council. I'll wake you once I have news."

It wasn't a suggestion, it was an order, and a man ordering me to go take a nap was about the only way I'd obey. I was fucking exhausted. I'd linked my power with the earth, seen the Blacks, and taken out a fog demon. And I still had to deal with Molly. All in a day's work.

"Alright ... but wake me the second the council has an answer ... or if Molly gets worse."

He nodded. "Promise." Leaning forward, he placed a kiss on my lips and gave me a playful nudge toward the house.

I wasn't about to object, and shuffled up the steps to the porch and down the hall before shutting myself in our bedroom. The bed looked so fucking comfortable I could cry. I kicked off my boots and shrugged out of my pants. Walking over to my side of the bed, I was about to crash into it when the small ring box on the nightstand caught my eye.

The ring.

The proposal.

I'd forgotten all about it, and seeing the box brought a smile to my lips.

Brock wanted to marry me.

Sitting down on the bed, I couldn't wait any longer. I peeled open the box, and right away emotion tightened in my throat. The ring was made of a thin band of white gold, with a giant amethyst set in the middle of it. A row of small diamonds encircled the stone.

Purple. My magic, my eyes. Brock had gotten me a ring that matched me! It was so incredibly thoughtful and unique and totally my style. The amethyst was super shiny and huge, at least four carats. I didn't want to know how much he'd spent on it. I simply loved it and I had to try it on. Pulling it from the box, I slipped it onto my ring finger and grinned. It was a perfect fit. Collapsing onto the bed, I stared up at my hand in awe.

Mrs. Evie Adams. Mrs. Evie Black-Adams. Hmm.

I was grinning like a fool, but sleep was pulling at the edges of my mind. I didn't want to take the ring off, so I didn't. I fell asleep with that huge fucker on my finger.

I was totally marrying Brock Adams. I just hadn't told him yet.

10 BITE ME

"EVIE..." Brock's smooth, deep voice dove into my consciousness, stirring me from a deep sleep. "Evie," he repeated, shaking me gently.

"Hmm...?" I mumbled.

Remembering all the shit that had gone down recently, my eyes popped open wide at the fact that Molly, who was like a little sister to me, was possessed by a fucking fog demon. Sure, maybe it was only a little part of the fog demon, but it was still more than enough. Images of her snarling and growling at us flashed through my mind, and I pushed myself up to a sitting position, rubbing at my face.

"How long was I asleep?" I asked Brock, before realizing he wasn't looking at me anymore. Well, not exactly. He was staring at my hand with full-on intensity.

A quick glance told me that I'd fallen asleep with the ring on my finger. *Shit.* This wasn't how I wanted him to find out I was accepting his proposal. I'd wanted to

LUCÍA ASHTA & LEIA STONE

declare it romantically—and not in the middle of this shitstorm with Molly.

When I looked back up, he was waiting for me, his amber eyes alight. "Does this mean what I think it means?" he asked.

I hesitated. "I don't want to do this when things are so messed up with Molly. First, tell me, do you have news?"

He nodded, his gaze once more flickering toward my engagement ring, a slight smirk pulling at his lips. "The council's vote was unanimous. I have their permission to turn Molly. They took a while to come to an agreement though." He grimaced, but with the dark stubble on his face, it only made him look dangerous and sexy. "You slept for more than three hours."

"How's Molly?" I insisted.

Brock scowled deeply, and even before he answered I knew I wouldn't like what he had to say.

"There's no way to sugarcoat it. She's not doing well. She's grown even more hostile than she was before, and now she's also refusing water and food. She looks like she's strung out."

I scooted toward the edge of the bed, slipped back into my pants, and bent over to pull on my boots. "We need to turn her right away, then. We can't wait."

"Can't it wait long enough for you to give me an answer? Are you going to marry me, Evie?"

Still seated on the bed, with my second boot half on, I turned to look at him. The stress of the demon fog and all the other terrifying shit that had emerged from the gate to the underworld was evident in the tension that rode his shoulders, the way his eyes crinkled in the corners with exhaustion. Brock was responsible for an entire pack, and he seemed to worry about me and the baby constantly. He didn't need to also worry about this.

I finished pulling on my boot and scooted closer to him on the bed, reaching for him, my ring glimmering across our joined hands. Staring into his eyes, I recognized all the hope he held for a beautiful future together, the love he had for me. Without a doubt, this was the man I wanted to share the rest of my life with.

Smiling, I leaned forward. "Yes, Brock Adams, I will marry you"—he broke into a grin that erased all the evidence of strain from his face—"*but*, I'm going to put the ring, which I totally love by the way, back in its box."

His forehead scrunched into lines of confusion. "I don't understand."

"You proposed to me while we were in the middle of dodging the Akuma and figuring out how to prevent what amounts to a demon apocalypse on earth. And you only did it when my dad freaked out about us living in sin. There's no fucking way I'm going to officially accept your proposal when my apprentice is fighting off demonic possession. We need good juju around this marriage."

I shook my long hair, the pitch black strands sliding across my bare upper arms. "No, we're going to do this right, once all this shit is over and the gate is sealed, taking with it all our nightmarish problems. Then you can wine and dine me, get down on one knee and look at me adoringly while you do your thing."

He chuckled. "I'll do whatever you want as long as you marry me."

"Absolutely whatever I want?" I asked, winking at him.

"Anything." His voice grew husky and his eyes hooded.

I let out the groan of all motherfucking groans. "Why can't we just have some time to be alone?"

"I've been asking myself that same thing basically since I met you."

"Before or after you parked a bulldozer in front of Gran's house and threatened to tear it down?"

"Yeah, definitely after that." He laughed, offering me his hand. "Come on, let's go get this over with."

Standing, I slid the ring from my finger, admiring it while I replaced it in its box, then took his hand.

"You're going to be stuck with me for the rest of our lives, Brock Adams," I told my alpha.

His eyes twinkled as he pulled me close, pressing a quick kiss to my waiting lips. "Lucky me," he said. "Now let's go make your apprentice a werewolf."

Well, that's not something you hear every day, I thought as I followed him from our bedroom and through the house. Then again, nothing about our lives had been ordinary since the moment we met. It probably never would be, though I'd settle for demon free.

I thought I'd imagined the worst when Brock told me Molly's condition had deteriorated, but nothing had prepared me for the malice that seemed to drip from her every pore. The moment Brock and I stepped through the threshold to Gran's cabin, Molly began to snarl and hiss like a wild animal.

She sat more or less on Gran's droopy, well-worn couch as she thrashed. Her ankles were bound with black silk bondage ties. I absolutely was not going to ask Haru or Reo how they'd come into possession of them to tie her up. The brothers and Molly had been living together in the cabin since I moved in with Brock, which meant they'd had plenty of opportunity to, uh, connect.

Haru and Reo knelt on the couch to either side of Molly, each of them gripping one of her arms tightly to keep her from hurting herself or anyone else. I could tell from the pained expressions on their faces that they were trying very hard not to harm her, but she wasn't making it easy.

As Brock and I approached, Molly lunged forward, half coming off the couch as she did, and Haru stumbled off the furniture while he and Reo tugged to hold her back.

"Don't bother trying to get close to her," Johnny said. "The person you knew isn't in control anymore, not at all."

I flicked an annoyed look at my cousin. The way he said it made it seem like we weren't getting Molly back, and we totally fucking were.

I looked to Cass, Tianna, Willemena, my dad, and Cho instead. Cass stepped forward, rubbing worriedly at his little potbelly. "We've got to hurry, Ev. The longer she's like this, the harder it will be for her to fight for control once she becomes a wolf."

Tianna nodded at her little impish lover. "He's right. If she stays this way much longer, she might start to forget who she really is, even once she's a wolf. We need to do this before any more damage can be done."

Brock released my hand and stalked forward. "Now that I have the council's approval, I don't need to wait anymore." He pulled up the hem of the form-fitting black t-shirt he wore, and when he yanked it over his head,

Cho's eyes went wide. Willemena and Tianna trained their eyes on him too, as if determined not to miss the show.

"Uh, Brock?" I said.

He looked up as he unsnapped his jeans. "Yeah?"

"Maybe you could undress in my old bedroom."

He scanned the witches, who were staring at him, as if noticing them for the first time, then moved into my old room, not bothering to close the door behind him.

Werewolves. They were so used to being naked around each other that they didn't give it much thought. It was the way their lives were. And it would soon be Molly's life.

I chewed my lip. I knew she wanted to be a supernatural and all, but would she be ready for coming out of this as a full-blown werewolf? And she would come out of this —because there was no way in hell I was even going to entertain the possibility that she might not survive the shift. She had to.

Cass, always so attuned to me, spoke into my thoughts: *'Don't worry, girl. Molly's strong. She'll pull through.'*

I nodded roughly. *'But will she be able to fight off this demon? Will she be the same carefree, supe-loving Molly we know?'*

'Of course she will.' But a hint of doubt crept across our telepathic link, making me shiver with dread before shaking it off.

Cass drew up to my side, offering his silent support. I could always count on my bestie to have my back, even when all I needed was some encouragement.

Brock padded out of my old room in wolf form just as Ray let himself into the cabin. When Brock met his second's gaze, I knew he'd been communicating with him through their pack link. He probably wanted Ray here just in case anything should go wrong.

No matter how many times I saw Brock's wolf, I couldn't help but admire it. The large gray wolf was all lean, muscled strength and fierce determination. Brock's yellow eyes moved from Ray to me, and I nodded.

It was time.

As if the fog demon within Molly understood what was about to happen, and what the end result of Brock's wolf bite would be, Molly thrashed and pulled against Haru and Reo's hold with such renewed ferocity that Ray and Johnny ran to help them contain her. Even my dad looked worried, rolling his wheelchair a little closer to my side. Willemena and Cho looked on with somber expressions, while Tianna crossed her arms over her chest and narrowed her eyes at the scene.

With Molly's arms pinned fully against the couch, she kicked her bound legs like a psychopathic mermaid. She bucked and sneered, gnashing and grinding her teeth so ferociously that I worried she might crack a tooth before this was all over.

But just as I was about to ask Cass and Tianna if they wanted to hold down her legs, Brock lunged for her. He was faster than I realized; he clamped sharp jaws around her bare leg, slicing into her calf without warning.

She roared in outrage, but Brock held on.

A fierce power whipped through our pack bond as his unseen alpha magic wrapped around Molly. His power was a tangible force sweeping like a gust of wind across the room. Tianna and Cho bristled, as if they too could feel the magic, then Molly flung her legs up in a brutal snap that dislodged Brock's jaw and sent him flying across the open living space. His wolf form crashed into a couple of dining room chairs, which toppled over like dominoes. Brock grunted, but twisted so that he somehow managed to land on four paws.

'Are you okay?' I asked him urgently through our pack link.

'Fine,' he grumbled. *'It's done. Now we just have to wait for the werewolf magic to spread into her and see if her body accepts it.'* Then he trotted off toward my old room again, and when he emerged, he was all hot man again.

If *her body accepts it. He said* if.

Brock ran a hand through his dark hair while we all took in Molly. Her resistance to the men holding her was decreasing, the fight appearing to ooze out of her like air out of a deflating balloon. When she finally sank against the couch in complete exhaustion, Johnny and Ray stepped away, and eventually even Haru and Reo released their hold on her, though they monitored her with narrowed eyes.

"How long will the transition take?" Tianna asked Brock.

"It depends on the person. It can take anywhere from a few minutes to a few hours. Since I'm an alpha and my magic is stronger, it will probably take less time. But I'm not sure what kind of effect the demon fog will have on things. That's new territory for me."

While everyone turned to stare at Molly again, whose purple-hair draped over the back of the couch, I studied Brock. His back was tense, his eyes sad.

'Are you all right?' I asked him privately, and he met my gaze across the room.

'Yeah, it's just that being a werewolf can be a risky life. And

she won't get a choice on which pack she's a part of either. Since I'm turning her, she'll automatically become part of my pack.'

'She trusts you,' I said. *'I'm sure she'll be glad not only to be a wolf, but to have you as her alpha.'* Croft wouldn't be too glad, but the vamp lawyer hadn't been coming around much anymore now that Molly had become part of our crew. Molly's days as his blood mistress were officially over, and I was damn glad. Ever since I'd known this girl, she'd wanted to be immersed in the supernatural world. She'd have no problem with the choice we'd made for her.

'I hope you're right,' Brock said. *'I hope she makes it through.'*

I didn't put words to how important it was for me that she make it through. I wouldn't lose Molly. No fucking way. I was not letting a damn fog demon take her from me. She *would* survive the turn. She had to. I'd accept nothing else.

Molly was unmoving, the contrast to her earlier behavior disturbing after she had fought for so many hours. She closed her eyes as if about to take a nap.

"Maybe we could have some tea while we watch her," Willemena suggested, already moving over to the dining table and righting the chairs Brock's wolf had crashed into.

Cass' head jerked up to meet mine and he grinned. I smiled back, my heart not quite in it, even though I could tell he was trying to cheer me up. "Tea is for pussies," he said, and Willemena whipped her head up.

She stared at Cass for several beats, before throwing her head back and laughing. Her long, gray hair was loose today, and it swept gracefully along her back as she laughed. Finally, she wiped at her eyes, and smiled sadly. "I miss Belinda."

I nodded. "I miss Gran too."

"I'm not sure this is the time to laugh and reminisce," Johnny said, narrowing his eyes at Willemena.

The old witch, who'd had Gran's trust, shrugged with disinterest, taking a seat with a sigh. "Son, someday you'll learn that you have to take life as it comes. You have to laugh when you can and roll with the punches. If you don't, this life will fucking break you."

Then Willemena tilted her head against the chair back and closed her eyes.

"I'll go put on a pot of coffee," Cass said, but stopped halfway to the kitchen when Molly sat straight up on the couch and screamed.

11 THIS BITCH HAS NINE LIVES

MOLLY'S CRY cut straight through my heart and had every single person in the cabin running toward her … and then stopping short when we realized there was nothing we could do to help her.

Her body contorted in every direction all at once, bones and cartilage crunching. Her face scrunched in pain, and a second scream ripped from her throat.

"Oh my God. What can we do?" I asked, panic rushing my words together.

Brock was already shaking his head sadly. "There's nothing we can do. She has to do this on her own—every wolf does. I'm surprised she started shifting this quickly, but now that she is, we'll find out soon enough if she's going to survive my wolf bite."

My pulse thudded loudly through my head, willing her to fight this with everything she had and pull through.

I lost track of how long I watched my purple-haired friend fight the way the wolf worked to shape her body into something it'd never been before. Sabine came and went, taking Molly's vitals and marking things on a clipboard. Somewhere along the line, Haru had untied Molly's ankles, and Cass had placed his stubby hand in mine, and we'd commiserated together. I didn't expect Johnny to stay this long, but he was still here. As was my father. We were all just looking on and waiting, hoping for the best. There was nothing else we could do.

After some time, I became almost numb to Molly's cries of pain. I had to push them away so they wouldn't make me crazy. Was this how it'd been when I'd first shifted into my fox? No wonder Cass had been so freaked out afterward.

Haru and Reo winced with each one of Molly's screams, until finally, after what seemed like an eternity, her cries lessened, and she simply whimpered. And when the whimpering ceased, a gorgeous white wolf with a black right front leg stood next to the couch, panting with exhaustion, ribcage heaving.

I'd half expected her fur to be purple.

Despite her physical exhaustion at the pain she'd had to endure, a steely strength blazed from her sky blue eyes.

'Our girl did it,' I whispered in awe to Cass through our connection. *'She fought and she made it.'*

'That she did.' I sensed Cass' proud grin even without turning to look at him. *'Our apprentice kicks some serious ass.'*

'You can say that again,' I said, then turned to find Brock grinning, his smile lighting up his whole face.

"Molly did it," he said aloud, and Tianna whooped so loudly that I startled before laughing to ease some of this ridiculous fucking tension.

The laughter of relief circled the room. Even Johnny

chuckled a couple of times before Molly yelped, and we all stopped celebrating.

"It's the demon," Cho and Willemena said in unison.

"Now we'll find out whether she has it in her to fight the demon and win," Tianna said, clenching her jaw and setting it into fierce lines, as if she were the one about to take on a fog demon instead of my apprentice.

"Molly," Johnny said, and the white wolf with the one black leg faced him, tilting her snout upward. "You have to fight the demon that's inside you. There's nothing we can do to help you. You have to get it out all on your own."

"You can do it, girl," Tianna encouraged. "You're a badass wolf. Now all you have to do is kick that demon's nasty ass back to the underworld."

Molly dipped her head; her shoulder muscles flinched as she seemed to take what the woman said to heart.

"That's it?" I whispered, meeting Tianna's gaze. "She just has to force it out and it goes back to the under-world?" I didn't want Molly to hear me and be discouraged.

My dad beat Tianna to the answer: "Not exactly. But once Molly evicts the demon, the witches and warlock will have to contain it, and either trap it back in the under-world by sending it through the gate, or obliterate it entirely."

"I'm all for obliterating it entirely," I mumbled.

"Hell yeah," Cass said. "Time to rid ourselves of this thing once and for all. There's no redemption for a fog demon. They're one of the darkest monsters of the under-world. We need to kill it."

"I can get on board with that plan," Tianna said, and cracked her knuckles.

"All right, Molly," I said loudly. "This part's on you. Kick some fog demon ass for all of us."

And that's exactly what Molly did.

After how torturous and prolonged her shift had been, I figured the fight with the demon would be similar. But Molly growled like her prey was right in front of her instead of inside her, and then narrowed her eyes in concentration until she started panting from the effort once more. After a few moments, a black, putrid-looking green mist rose from her fur.

Holy shit. She was doing it.

Haru and Reo's eyes widened as they drew closer to their girl, desperate for a way to assist and ease her struggle. But damn if Molly didn't have this all on her own.

She snarled and growled and grunted ... until every speck of nasty-ass fog had emerged from within her to hover just above her body.

When she collapsed against the floor in exhaustion, Haru and Reo swept forward to ease her into their arms, as Johnny, Tianna, Willemena, and Cho extended their arms above their heads. Cho began calling out some more rapid-fire Japanese. The power building in the room crackled across my skin. When Cho clapped her hands together, I jumped and squealed.

Damn, Cho was one badass witch. Gone was the pleasant, kind-looking Japanese caretaker. She looked like she could take on the entire underworld right now, her nostrils flaring, her jaw clenched with power.

Johnny, Willemena, and Tianna clapped their hands together immediately after Cho, and magic swept around them in a whoosh, creating a square of vibrating white light that pulsated between the four of them. The fog that had left Molly rushed toward the square of power they'd formed, apparently compelled by Cho's spell. The fog whipped into the center of their power square, bouncing around like a ball trying to escape a pinball machine.

But there was no escape.

"We expel you from this earthly plane!" Johnny called out.

"We nullify your power. You can do no more harm," Willemena said.

"We banish you from this world and transmute your essence to the white light of the universe," Tianna added.

"With our combined power, you cease to exist. Now!" Cho roared.

In precise synch, Cho, Tianna, Willemena, and Johnny clapped their hands once more ... and the dark fog vanished as if it had never been there at all.

Not a single trace of the demon fog remained as I trudged with heavy legs to an open chair and sank into it. That tiny little speck of fog demon had just taken four powerful witches to eliminate it. The monsters from the underworld were no joke.

Holy shit. We did it. And we'd all survived.

I slouched into the dining room chair. Molly was looking better already, all evidence of her struggle to shift and banish the demon fog gone. In its place was a wolfish grin.

My supe-groupie girl was now a supe herself. And she looked damn pleased about it.

Brock approached Molly and knelt before her, reaching out slowly. She lowered her head to her new alpha as he stroked her back. I could see in the way they were looking at each other that they were speaking mentally. Finally, Brock stood and addressed the room.

"If you'll excuse us, my new pup would like to go for a run. It will be easier for her to remain a wolf for the next day or so before turning back. Shifting expends a lot of energy, and I need to work on helping her control her wolf."

We were all grinning like mad. Molly and Brock running as wolves together? I wanted to pull out my camera and take a video because it was fucking perfect.

"Have fun," I told my man. "We'll get something for dinner and meet you back here."

Brock led Molly out the front door, and the moment he pulled it closed behind them, everyone collapsed onto the couch.

My cousin was the first to rub his belly. "Did you say dinner?"

I grinned. "I'll order pizza."

When I pulled out my phone, I realized I'd left it on silent since my nap and had about fifty missed calls from two different people: Croft and Detective Swanson.

Oh God. A stone sank in my stomach. Why would these two people be trying like mad to get a hold of me?

"Actually, Cass, you order the pizza," I said. "I'm gonna step outside and make a few calls."

My bestie nodded, though he cocked his brow at me because I usually put pizza first. I'd fill him in later. Right now I didn't know what was going on.

I walked pretty far out onto the front driveway so I could have privacy, and decided to call Detective Swanson back first. None of my callers had left a voicemail, which was definitely weird.

Detective Swanson picked up immediately. "Evie?"

"Hey. Sorry, my phone was off. Please tell me we don't have another fog demon trapped in town."

"No. It's worse."

"Worse?" I croaked. What the fuck was worse than what we'd just gone through?

The detective sighed. "Look, I just wanted to give you a heads-up since you've helped us so much. The fog demon story got national media coverage. Now there's going to be a press conference at the White House tonight."

The whole forest around me swam at his words and dizziness overtook me. National media coverage. White House press conference. Oh, this was so bad.

"Okay..." Supernatural shit made the news often, but when they called a press conference, a smackdown was coming.

"Evie, they're going to make every supernatural register for identification and adhere to curfew and God knows what else. They've had enough. I felt I owed you a heads-up since your crew helped us out of a bind. Teams will be heading out in the morning."

Identification, curfew. *What?* My hands shook as adrenaline pumped through me. Teams heading out?

"Thanks, Detective. I gotta run, but I really appreciate the heads-up," I told him and signed off.

I called Croft.

"Do you know?" I asked the second the vampire answered.

"That the government is about to tag us like animals and attempt to control our every move? Yes, I have an inside source."

Fuck!

"What do we do?" I asked. He was the leader of the local vampire seethe, and a lawyer. If anyone had a plan, it'd be him.

"It's too late for us," he replied, "but as far as the authorities know, you're human. So while we're all getting registered starting tomorrow, you remain human. Do you understand?"

Holy shit. My head swam with the ramifications. I was registered at birth as a human, and when I'd starting working with Mack, I'd enlisted as a human. Every bounty hunter's race had to be listed on their application.

"Okay. Human. Got it. Anything else?" I said while my brain galloped off in a million different directions. This was really bad. Increased control was the first step in a war for race supremacy.

Heavy silence descended upon our conversation until Croft finally spoke again. "Anyone demonic in origin is going to be taken to a holding site until they can determine the individual's role in society."

Bile rose in my throat.

Cass. They were coming for Cass. For my best friend in the whole entire world, the one who always had my back.

Over my dead fucking body.

That little booty-short-wearing demon imp was no danger to humans.

I whimpered.

Croft cleared his throat. "So tomorrow morning when the registration team arrives at the alpha's place, you have no supernaturals of demon origin on your property."

Oh God.

"Damn right I don't." My voice shook.

"And Evie?"

I swallowed hard. "What?"

"Close that fucking gate," he said, and hung up.

I was really glad I took that three-hour nap, because shit was about to hit the fan.

12 I WILL FUCKING CUT YOU

I DIDN'T HAVE the composure to deal with the upcoming shitstorm calmly after what had just happened to Molly. My nerves were frayed. So instead of walking into the cabin and coolly announcing that we had an issue to talk about, I ran through the door and yelled that the government was coming after us and Cass was going to be taken. Needless to say, it created a panic.

Tianna was fierce. "So they're coming in the morning?" An unseen wind blew through her hair, causing it to fly off her shoulders as her magic whipped around her. She stood in front of Cass like a sentinel.

Johnny stood from his place at the table. "That means they'll be coming for us too."

I nodded. "Detective Swanson said in the morning. You'd better go prepare the coven."

My cousin nodded and started for the door, but as he reached me he placed a hand on my shoulder. "This was crazy, no doubt about it, but it was still nice to see you after so long."

I smiled. "Thanks for all your help."

With a quick bob of his head, Johnny was out the door. One of the wolves would give him a ride back to Cottage Grove.

Brock was still out on his run with Molly and I didn't have the heart to call him back just yet. I needed to figure this out first.

Cass stepped out from behind Tianna. "If they want me, they can try to come and get me. They won't like what happens." He crossed his arms over his little potbelly and scowled.

My heart pinched. Cass was a badass for sure, but I didn't think he was a match for the entire human government.

Kneeling down, I met his gaze. "I'm sure you could lay a good ass whooping on anyone who came after you, but eventually they'd find you. They might even kill you if you seem like you're causing trouble."

His frown intensified. "I don't care."

Tianna reached down and smoothed the pink furry hair between his horns. "I care, hot stuff. We can't let that happen."

I nodded. "And we're sure as hell not going to. I have an idea..."

Cass' eyes grew wide. "I know that look. No! Last time you had that look I nearly lost my finger." He pushed a stubby finger into the air, waving it around.

I chewed on my lip. "It'll be temporary. Just while the agents are here registering everyone. Once they leave, you can come out of hiding."

Cass leveled me with a suspicious gaze. "Hiding where?"

I was pretty sure the humans were smart enough to bring along supernatural agents, probably witches, to sniff out all supernaturals on the property and make certain everyone was accounted for and registered. The only way to properly hide Cass while the agents were in town was to...

"Hide just inside the gate," I mumbled.

Tianna's eyes widened so far I thought they might fall out. "The gate to the underworld!"

I winced. "Well, yeah. No one else can see it and Cass can go in there, unlike the rest of us, so it seems like the best hiding spot."

"Best hiding spot if we want him to be eaten by a fog demon!" Tianna roared. "Or something worse!"

Cho, my father, the Japanese warriors, Willemena, and Ray all just watched us bicker while they remained silent.

"She's right," Cass said.

I was?

"I can slip into the gate and go undetected if they search the property magically, which I'm sure they will. If the government is getting involved, they'll be smart about things. I'll find a good hiding spot and lay low for the day. You guys can send in some type of signal when it's safe to return."

Tianna looked so vulnerable right then I thought she might cry. Seeing the fierce Amazonian fae-witch like this was worse than her rage.

"I can get a flare gun," I said. "Shoot it through when it's safe."

Tianna rolled her eyes. "Do you want to alert half of the underworld to Cass' presence? No, I'll send a magical signal that only he will hear."

Oh yeah, that was way better.

Tianna frowned. "But I don't want you going in there alone."

Cass thought about it. "I might not have to. Let me check in with a friend. I'll be back." He started for the door. "T baby, you're with me."

I smiled as Tianna shuffled after her man, glad we'd found a quick solution.

"Text me if anything happens!" I screamed after my bestie.

When I turned to check in with the others and make a plan, my father was right there, in my face.

"Evie, if they're registering supernaturals..."

I nodded. "I know. They'll probably have witches and sniff me out."

His eyes brimmed with concern. "We can't let anyone find out what you are. It will lead the Akuma straight to you."

Fuck. I'd forgotten about the damn Akuma again. The sirens were off in the underworld and the Akuma hadn't shown up since.

"How can I hide what I am?" I pressed my father. If these government officials had witches capable of sniffing me out or forcing me to shift, there was nothing I could do to conceal my true nature from them. They'd have a field day if they figured out I was a kitsune.

Cho sidled next to my dad. "I have an idea. I can create a potion that will keep her from shifting or smelling like a shifter for twenty-four hours, no matter the circumstances, and it won't harm the baby."

"That way, worst case, she'll just look like a mediocre witch," Haru interjected.

That was a bit too close to home after my history of being the Black family dud, but it sounded like our best plan.

"It's worth a try," I told Cho.

After a curt nod, she climbed the stairs to Gran's loft, where all the tincture-making items were kept.

Now that we had a plan in place, I couldn't put off telling Brock any longer.

'Hey, umm ... can you guys head back early? We've got some news.'

His energy bristled across our link. *'Ray just told me. I've called a pack meeting.'*

My eyes flicked across the room to Ray.

Tattle.

Brock's second-in-command shrugged as if to say that was his job.

A pack meeting? That sounded serious. Brock wasn't going to try to fight this ... was he?

"We're going to fight this!" Brock roared as he stood on his back porch an hour later and looked out across the grim faces of over a hundred pack members.

Oh God.

"Most of you have jobs in town and work odd hours. A curfew could keep you from making your night shifts. An ID tag could get you fired if your boss doesn't know you're a wolf."

The men and women in the crowd were nodding.

'Just what do you expect to do to fight this?' I asked my alpha privately.

He turned to meet my gaze, but answered aloud. "I have a meeting with the local vampire seethe leader. We are going to come up with a plan by morning that makes sure this new law won't interfere with your livelihood."

The pack roared their agreement, and then Brock looked back at me. *'Want to go meet Croft with me?'*

'Hell yes.' If my man and the local king of the vampires were going to be making some plan for rebellion, then I wanted to be involved.

The drive to meet Croft was filled with anxiety. Cho was making me some freaking anti-shifting potion, Cass was trying to meet up with some demon buddy so he didn't have to hide out in the underworld alone, and I was pretty sure Brock was about to flip his shit on the American government.

"So what are you thinking?" Croft asked Brock as he paced the length of his private office.

We were in the vampire's law firm, the very one I'd come to after my gran had died so that I could get my inheritance.

Brock splayed his big hands out on Croft's desk. "As leaders, we throw ourselves under the bus. We follow curfew and let them tag us, but we tell them they won't be touching our pack or seethe. We make a full-on threat. Half of my pack runs this town from positions of power."

Croft stopped pacing and grinned. "You think they'll listen?"

Brock shrugged. "This is a small town. If I pull all my

wolves from their human jobs, it will damn near shut the place down."

The big vampire rubbed his chin. "I've got two ER doctors in my seethe. If I pull them, people will die."

I gasped. "You have vampires working around bloody, injured humans?"

Croft nodded. "They are old and can control their bloodlust." He returned his attention to Brock. "I've also got over a hundred blood slaves on monthly retainer."

Yeah, Molly was one of them. *Was* being the keyword.

"So we blackmail them." I had to say it aloud, because it was crazy.

Croft nodded. "We blackmail them. It won't work in the bigger cities, but in Eugene, Oregon, we might just get away with it. For the time being, anyway."

Brock stood and shook Croft's hand. "Thank you for the consult. I'll keep you apprised of the situation in the morning."

Croft nodded. "And I will do the same."

As Brock and I walked out to the car, I turned to him and he stopped. "What happens if they say no? If they ... try to identify everyone and ... tag them by force?"

The muscles in his jaw ticked. "We're drawing a line in the sand. If they cross it, they'll be declaring war with the supernaturals, and I don't think they'll want that."

I gulped.

"I've been cleared by the council to use lethal force if necessary to get the point across," he added. "The werewolves are half human, and we won't be abiding by these archaic rules of theirs."

Damn. He was right. But I had a really bad feeling about this.

13 OH HELL

WE SPENT the rest of the night figuring out how to best prepare for the human agents scheduled to descend upon us the next day in a "surprise" registration visit. If it hadn't been for my well-placed friends and colleagues, the registration squad might have caught us with our proverbial pants around our ankles. As it was, we were as ready as we'd get.

Willemena had been the first to take off. Her home in California was entirely off the grid, and so deep in the forest that nobody would be able to locate it without insider information. Since Willemena closely guarded her secrets, she was certain the human agents would never be able to find her, and even if they somehow managed it, they'd need to overcome her impenetrable wards. Preferring her odds alone than in the company of more than a hundred supes, the crone had laid rubber in her sleek back Porsche 911 Carrera, barely bothering with brief goodbyes. I couldn't help but like her despite her gruff demeanor. When shit got rough, she had our backs, and that's all that mattered.

Haru, Reo, Molly, and Tianna had left after her to spend the night with the Blacks out at Cottage Grove. Johnny had surprised me by calling and offering my friends sanctuary.

In the eyes of the human authorities, the only thing more dangerous than a supe was a lone, rogue supe, especially one who didn't fit neatly into their boxes. Tianna wasn't associated with a coven, so she'd fare better connected to the Black Clan, and Cho insisted that Haru and Reo would benefit from its protection as well. I'd long suspected that the Japanese warriors weren't entirely human, and Cho more or less confirmed it. There was no way we could allow unfriendly witches to start prodding around what and who the brothers were. My identity as the last remaining kitsune on earth had to remain a secret at all costs.

When Haru and Reo had protested, not wanting to leave Molly behind, Brock had suggested she go with them. As a new wolf, Molly was a bit unstable, and it would be better to keep her from being too closely examined. Johnny was slick, and I had no doubt he'd come up with any necessary reasons to explain away their presence among them. We'd debated sending Cass with them as well, instead of into the underworld. It was possible the police might not bother with Cottage Grove at all since the Blacks were an established coven, but with the recent news that the Blacks were delving in dark magic, it was more likely the cops would be all over them.

My dad and Cho were tucked away in Gran's cabin. When I asked Cho if she wasn't worried about being pegged as a lone witch herself, and if it wouldn't be better to go to Cottage Grove with the others, she'd said she couldn't shirk her duty to care for my father. She'd insisted she could take care of herself, and after the displays I'd seen from her, I wasn't inclined to argue. As far as witches went, she was the bee's knees, and it touched me that she would choose to remain at my father's side.

In the early morning hours, Cass slipped into the underworld and was now safely hidden away, though I wasn't even close to feeling comfortable about his location. He'd enlisted the demon bartender, who worked at the bar where Brock and I'd first met, to go along with him. I couldn't help but worry about the variety of things that could happen to Cass there, but at least this way he was guaranteed to escape the human agents. There was no way I'd stand by and allow them to take Cass away from me and put him in some all-demon concentration camp.

We'd been forced to reveal the existence of the gate to the demon bartender, but we'd had no choice. At least he didn't know I was a kitsune and the guardian to the gate, and he'd appreciated a heads-up about the feds being after his kind. He and Cass seemed to have struck up a little friendship even though I thought he was a douchebag. After twenty minutes of searching for the crack in the gate that would allow Cass and the bartender entrance, Cass had given up and ferried the bartender away to the other side of the property while I'd shifted to my kitsune form. Short of flooding Brock's property the way Calista had, the only way to find the exact opening was with my kitsune sight.

Before I transformed, I'd only had to shift two more times to gain my nine tails so I could seal the gate for good. Now we were down to one more time. My shift to my fox form had come a bit easier, the transformation taking less time and forcing me to endure less pain. That was a big win. I'd also developed an eighth power. I could now tell the exact time just by looking at the sky, night or day. Yeah, I know, not super useful, but with how crazy my life was, there was always a chance the skill could get us out of a scrape—somehow—and now I'd never need a watch again.

When I'd signaled the location of the crack in the gate to Brock, he'd marked it with a construction flag. By the time Cass brought the demon bartender back, I was back to looking like a pregnant human. With repeated promises that I'd come for Cass the moment the agents were gone, my pink furry demon imp bestie jumped into the gate and vanished from sight.

Getting everyone organized yesterday had made for an incredibly long day, and today Brock and I were up at the butt crack of dawn so the agents couldn't get the jump on us. Even so, we'd barely made it out to the lawn when we noticed the first signs of their approach.

I checked my supernatural bounty hunter badge, clipped at my waist, and my Glock, to make sure they were in place. Though Brock had begged me to hide out with the Blacks, or even in the house or Gran's cabin, I'd refused. There was no way in hell I was going to allow Brock to face a horde of humans on his own. Besides, the human authorities respected supernatural bounty hunters. When they needed help bringing down a supe, we were the ones they called. My presence would ensure they wouldn't take things too far with Brock.

Or so I hoped.

There weren't many laws in place that protected paranormals. I intended to make the most of the few that did. The humans were within their lawful right to identify and register all supernaturals, but they couldn't force us to do anything beyond that unless they could prove we were somehow an imminent threat to a human. Being fond of rule bending myself, I didn't trust these agents for a second. Once humans started looking at us as outsiders and a potential threat to their existence, there was no telling what they'd do.

"Can you tell if the potion worked?" Brock asked, cracking his neck and knuckles while narrowing his eyes at the caravan of military-grade armored vehicles steadily making their way down the road to our house.

Was that level of military presence really necessary?

"I don't feel any different," I said. "But I trust Cho. If she says it'll make me appear nothing more than a weak witch to any other supes, it should be enough for them not to pay attention to me. And she said the potion definitely took effect. She didn't pick up on my shifter side at all."

Brock didn't say anything, clenching his jaw at the approaching convoy.

"Don't you trust Cho?" I pressed.

"I trust Cho. It's the assholes driving over-equipped Hummers onto my residential property that I'm inclined to distrust."

He was right. Hummers, especially armored and reinforced ones like the ones headed our way, were way over the top for an innocent registration assignment. I took a step closer to Brock and he immediately wrapped a protective arm around my waist.

"Are you sure I can't convince you to wait inside?" he asked.

"Not a chance."

He growled under his breath but didn't press the issue. We waited in silence until the first of the vehicles slid to a stop at the edge of our driveway. The large Hummers were definitely military grade, machines of war disguised in quasi-civilian shells.

Brock stood tall, pinning a searing gaze on the man approaching us. The soldier was dressed in black army fatigues, with enough weapons strapped to his body to make me jealous. Two men and a witch hopped out of the vehicle after him and flanked him.

"You'd better have a damn good reason to come onto my property like this," Brock snarled.

"I do." The lead agent offered Brock some ID. "I'm Field Agent Maler, and my team and I are here to do a routine inspection of the premises, including any supernaturals you might have living here."

"Routine? Bullshit," Brock growled. "I know exactly why you're here."

Agent Maler cocked a brow at that and ignored Brock. "Due to the new law passed late last night, I am now required to register every supernatural on the premises."

"I didn't hear about a new law," Brock said coolly. The White House press release just said they were drafting a law that would address the issue.

The man gave a sinister grin. "We kept it under wraps so as to prevent panic among supernaturals."

More like to prevent supes from escaping before the agents arrived. I barely held back my own growl, and I only managed it because I knew I couldn't do anything to suggest I was anything but an innocuous witch growing a baby.

A witch stepped forward, a clipboard in her hands. "State your name for the record." She was all business. And powerful. I could feel it.

"I'm Brock Adams," Brock said. "I'm the owner of this land, and alpha of the local werewolf pack."

Brock wasn't the owner of Gran's cabin and her property, but now wasn't the time to make that point.

"I demand to know why you've brought such a military show of force," Brock pressed. "Your entourage doesn't exactly look gentle and innocent. My pack has done nothing wrong."

Four more Hummers had pulled in behind the first, and from each descended another team of soldiers accompanied by one witch. The soldiers all wore identical army fatigues, an admirable array of weapons, buzz cuts, and impassive expressions. The only women among them were the witches, and even they seemed hard as steel. Witches tended to be a colorful lot with boisterous personalities, but not this crew. If looks could cut me down, I'd be rolling on the ground.

"We're here to perform a census of all supernaturals on the premises," Agent Maler said.

"And by 'census,' do you mean tag us so you can track our every movement?" Brock asked, his arm squeezing around my back at his building anger.

The agent met Brock's challenging stare without blinking. "Yes. Our orders are to install a nano tracking device in every supernatural on the premises. Like I said, it's the new law, and every supernatural must comply."

Brock's jaw twitched as pissed-off nervous flutters raced through me. This dude was talking about us like we were cattle!

"I refuse," Brock said, his voice deadly calm.

Shit was about to hit the fan.

"If you refuse, then my orders are to proceed with force." For the first time, Agent Maler directed his attention at me. "And who are you?" He trailed his eyes across my badge and weapon.

I held my head high. "I'm Evie Black, licensed supernatural bounty hunter. I'm here in an official capacity to make sure you adhere to the law."

"An official capacity? Really?" He pointedly looked at the way Brock held on to me like his efforts alone could keep me safe.

"Yes," I said, deadpan.

Fuck you, agent man.

"She's also my fiancée," Brock said. "Which means you keep your hands off her or you'll have me to deal with."

I'd never been frightened of Brock, but right then, if I were the agent, I'd be terrified. Menace dripped off of Brock's every word.

But Agent Maler didn't so much as wince. "I have a job to do, and I intend to do it." He signaled for his people to move forward, and they all started to walk at once, crowding around him. Even the witches appeared to be waiting for him to give the next order.

"Listen to me very, very carefully," Brock grit out. "I'm not going to allow you to tag everyone in my pack. There's no way in hell. We're not animals."

Agent Maler opened his mouth to protest, but Brock continued before he could. "But I understand you need to follow orders, so I'll offer you a compromise. I'll allow you to tag me and I'll be personally responsible for the actions of every single member of my pack. I can sign whatever papers you want legally binding me to take the fall for anything my pack members do."

My heart was thumping somewhere up in my throat. I got that Brock trusted his wolves and had faith in them, but putting himself on the line for anything they might do ... that was nuts. What if one of his wolves lost control? Even the most well behaved wolf went wild on the full moon.

"I can't accept your offer," Agent Maler said. "I have to tag every wolf on the property. Are there any other supernaturals on the premises? Besides your pack?"

The witches looked at me with suspicion. Brock ignored his question. "I have more than a hundred wolves in my pack. They hold important positions in the community. Most of the town don't even know they're supes because they appear human. If you push me on this, not only will we fight you, but I'll order every one of my wolves to go on strike. A town like this will shut down without my wolves. I have everything from doctors and teachers to librarians and mechanics and firefighters. My wolves are hard workers, and they're involved in almost everything that goes on in this town."

"No one cares about what happens in a town like this," Agent Maler said.

"I highly doubt that," Brock said. "Especially when I have the approval of the National Werewolf Council. They've agreed to abide by this strike with me. How will your superiors feel about a nationwide strike by the wolves? That will mean thousands of critical employees absent from daily human life. A wolf strike will send dominoes crashing on all sides. Oh, and did I mention? I'm also friends with the vampires, the supernaturals that line your government's politician's pockets. They have agreed to go on strike with us. Seems to me you didn't think this out very well."

I wasn't sure Croft would consider Brock a friend, but whatever. This Agent Maler needed to back the fuck off, and I could see hesitation in his face.

"With that much momentum," Brock continued, "the entire supernatural community would go on strike in protest of these unconstitutional measures. Not to mention it would start a civil war."

"Even the bounty hunters would," I piped up. "And then you'd have nobody to call on to help you subdue supes."

The lead agent huffed, frustration sweeping across his steely features. "My superiors won't approve this. My orders are clear!"

"Your orders are bullshit. Do you want to start a war?" I asked. "Call your superiors."

Brock nodded. "Tell them I'll cooperate and allow them to track *me*, but that's it. If they press the issue, they'll have a war with supes on their hands."

The soldiers behind Agent Maler shot furtive looks between Brock, me, and their leader. Finally, Agent Maler pulled a cell phone from one of the many pockets on his fatigues. "Watch them," he barked to his team while walking out of hearing range. Every soldier there, including the witches, moved closer, making me feel like my skin was crawling.

A couple of the witches started sniffing the air, directing pointed looks at me. I plastered what I hoped was a look of complete innocence across my face. They only narrowed their eyes at me.

Shit. Cho's potion had better work.

Just as one of the witches was inching closer, Agent Maler returned, his phone still held to his ear. "I have to at least take down the names of everyone on the property," he called out to Brock.

"But I'm the only one who gets tagged?" Brock asked.

Maler gave a curt, displeased nod.

"Agreed."

"He's agreed, sir," Maler spoke into the cell phone. He listened for a few more seconds before disconnecting. When his gaze traveled between Brock and me, I knew without a doubt that this man would have loved to install tracking devices in every single one of us.

"My supervising officer has agreed," Maler said, "but only for now. We'll be revisiting the issue at a later date."

"Then let's get this over with," Brock growled. "I have far better things to do with my morning."

Maler tipped his head to a soldier behind him, and a man with sandy blond hair growing low on his forehead went to retrieve a metal briefcase from the nearest vehicle. He pulled out a scary-ass contraption with a huge, long needle attached to it.

"You can't let him inject you with that," I whispered urgently to Brock.

"I have to," he said, extracting his arm from my side. He approached the soldier while pulling his shirt over his head and offering him his bare shoulder. "I take it that it doesn't matter where you inject the tracker?"

"No, sir," the soldier said.

"Good. Then let's get it done."

An alcohol swab and thirty seconds later, my future husband could be tracked by the US government anywhere, at any time. Not a single aspect of this was sitting well with me.

The three witches stepped forward then and clasped hands. "We've been ordered to do a quick spell to hunt out any demons you may have on the property. This is non-negotiable."

Panic ripped through me, but I kept my face calm. Thank God we'd gotten Cass into hiding. I just hoped the gate kept him hidden or we were in for a world of trouble. Brock nodded, and the three witches started to chant.

I recognized immediately that they were doing a power of three spell. I'd seen Gran do a few of them outside in the back yard with her friends. They were powerful and little could hide from them.

Please let Cass be okay.

A white mist rolled out from their hands and shot out across Brock's land in one quick burst.

The head witch raised an eyebrow. "No living demons on the property, but there has been one here recently. The essence still lingers."

Fuck!

"Yeah, the entire town just fought a fog demon," Brock interjected.

Thank God for his quick thinking, because I'd had no idea what to say.

128

The woman nodded her understanding, and the witches broke apart.

"My second-in-command has a full list of every single wolf under my authority," Brock announced to the agent in charge. "He's bringing it out to you now."

On cue, Ray emerged from the house, a sheaf of papers clutched in one hand.

"That won't be acceptable," Agent Maler said. "We need to take down their names in person and confirm them with their state-issued IDs."

Brock crossed his arms over his chest and glared. "The list is all I can offer at this time." A patch of fur worked its way up Brock's arms and the lead agent's eyes widened a little.

Maler's jaw worked, and when Ray handed over the papers, he snatched them out of his hands and stared at my man. "This isn't over, Brock Adams. It's far from over."

Brock's lips curved into a frigid, deadly smile. "You can count on it."

When Maler stomped back to the lead Hummer, the soldiers and witches under his command followed suit. Within minutes, they'd all peeled out of the driveway, leaving clouds of dust—and a shitload of anxiety—in their wake.

14 FUCK YOU, AGENT FUCKFACE

I WAS FAR from happy about how things had gone down with Agent Fuckface, but at least it was over—for now. The first thing I did once the convoy of trucks faded from sight was hightail it to the site of the gate. With the flag marker, it was easy to locate the part of the gate that was cracked open—making sure I didn't fall straight through. Because I'd consumed Cho's potion, I wouldn't be able to shift for twenty-four hours. Not that I would want to anyway; I needed to take it slow for the baby's sake.

"Cass! It's safe to come out," I yelled, pulling up Tianna's contact listing on my phone. I knew we'd agreed that she'd come up with a spell that would go into the gate and notify him it was safe to return, but I couldn't discount the possibility that he might be able to hear me and come out on his own. No point making things complicated if we didn't need to. The less time my bestie spent in the underworld, the better.

"Cass!" I called again right as Tianna answered her phone. "Hey," I said to her while Brock filed in behind me.

"The agents just left. I'm calling to Cass, but I'm not sure he can hear me. You should probably head out here to do your spell once you're all clear over there."

"I can't," she said, voice tight. "I'm trapped here."

"What?" I squeaked. "Is everyone all right? What's going on?"

Tianna chuckled. "No need to freak out, girl. We're all fine. So fine that the agents skipped right over us. Johnny did some kind of last-minute high-level cloaking spell that disguised the location of the entire coven. We saw the armored vehicles driving by on the road, but they couldn't find us."

"No doubt they intended to surprise us all at once so we couldn't warn each other," Brock grumbled from where he was listening to the conversation at my side.

"That was smart," I said to Tianna.

"A little too smart maybe," Tianna said. "It was such an advanced spell that Johnny is having a bit of trouble taking it down now, and I've never seen anything like it before. We're trying to figure out what's glitching. The cloaking sort of backfired and locked us in at the same time. No one can leave the property."

"So you might be a while, then?" I asked.

"Seems like it. I'm sure we'll get it figured out with time."

"All right ... well, I'll just keep calling to Cass until you can get here. He should be fine to wait in there a little longer."

"Uh, Evie," Brock said, and I spun to face the direction of the gate.

"Hold up," I spoke into the phone. "The bartender is climbing out of the gate."

"Hey, man," Brock called out.

The large demon bartender, who'd come on to me when I first met him, was grim. His face looked ashen, and his mouth was pulled into a frown.

"What is it?" I asked, my heart thumping in my chest already. That was the face of someone with bad fucking news to share.

"They took Cass," the bartender with the horns said in a gruff voice.

"What do you mean, 'they took Cass?'" I was going to be sick.

"They came out of nowhere and snatched him before we had the chance to react. They snuck up on us, knocked me out."

"What the hell is going on?" Tianna asked through the phone, but I couldn't answer her yet.

I forced the words through a throat that was suddenly bone dry. "Who's 'they?' Who took him?"

"Three sirens. We didn't even see them coming."

"Tianna," I snapped into the phone, "get that spell down as quickly as you fucking can. We've got a big problem over here and I'll take all the help I can get. These bitch sirens have Cass, and I'm getting him back. And then I'm going to kill every motherfucking one of them."

"What's happening to her?" Brock asked my father with panic in his voice. I was pacing the living room floor; arcs of purple magic flared off my skin, lashing out at the walls and leaving dark marks there.

"She is angry, and her magic is becoming unstable." My father spoke as if I wasn't there. I knew I needed to calm down, that weird shit was happening to my body, but I couldn't. My best friend in the entire world had been taken. Calista and her psychotic evil sisters had turned my life into a shit show and I was pissed. If one tiny pink hair on his head was damaged, I would eviscerate them all.

"Ev. Can you focus on my voice?" Brock said quietly.

I stopped pacing. "I can hear you," I snapped. "I'm trying." Then I resumed my pacing.

I couldn't go into the gate because it would kill me. I wasn't demon in origin. I didn't have any demon bounty hunter friends or anyone I could send in after Cass, and while the bartender was willing to help as much as he could, let's face it, he was a fucking bartender—useless in a fight against three nasty bitches.

A crash pulled my attention as a painting ripped off the wall and slammed onto the floor.

Shit.

My purple magic was like a violent whip right now, and I didn't know how to fix it. "Whoops. Sorry," I winced.

"Evie," Brock snapped. "You could be hurting our baby!"

Fear flushed through me, dousing my anger; the purple streaks finally subsided. My hands shook as Brock's face swam into view.

"I'm sorry." Tears lined my eyes. "Cass ... my sweet Cass."

"We'll find him. I promise." Brock rubbed my arms and then looked at Cho and my father. Normally this room would be full of people, but we were down to a group of four.

"Has anything like this ever happened to you before? The ... magic flying out?" My alpha was clearly worried, and now I felt awful for how I'd lost it. I needed to get better control over myself.

My gaze flicked to my father, who answered Brock: "The anger streak was usually her mother's thing. But it happened to me once or twice too. Completely normal, but not exactly safe when you have power lashing out with no intention."

Shame colored my cheeks. "I'm so sorry everyone ... I was seeing red, I couldn't control it."

My father wheeled closer to me. "It's perfectly normal. Someone you love has been taken." Reaching up, he clasped my hand and I bent on one knee to face him.

"Dad—" That word still felt weird in my mouth. "Help me get Cass. You have to have an idea, a way inside. I know I'm not a demon, but there has to be a spell or something that could help." My gaze flicked to Cho as the panic ramped higher. How long had it been since he'd been taken? Were they hurting him? I wasn't able to mind message him at the gate, so he must be far away. How would I find him?

Cho shook her head. "There's no spell that could temporarily turn you into a demon that wouldn't also risk you and the child."

I was going to be sick. We had to get Tianna out of the Black coven's land. She would be able to help me ... maybe.

Fuck!

My father rubbed his chin. "I have a thought."

Hope burst inside my chest. "Tell me."

"Haru was telling me that you'd formed a bit of an

alliance with the selkies. And selkies are creatures of the underworld."

Creatures of the underworld.

The entire room spun as adrenaline coursed through me. The selkies! Yes.

"Dad, that's genius!"

Brock cleared his throat. "Umm ... you do remember that before we left the cove, the selkie leader almost didn't let us go, right?"

Yeah, well, technicalities. We all wanted the same thing. For me to close the gate and for the Akuma to go fuck themselves.

"Brock, if they could help us get Cass ... we have to try," I said.

He sighed. "You're right. I'll charter a helicopter. Call Tianna one more time, see if she's made any headway on breaking out of the Black's land."

I nodded. This was going to work. It had to.

Tianna picked up on the first ring. "Tell me good news."

"You first," I prodded.

She sighed heavily into the phone. "We're fucking stuck here. Your cousin has even called in some friends to break down the spell from the outside, but they can't fucking find us. We're definitely going to be here a while."

No.

"Can you like, shatter it or do another pentacle spell or something?" I suggested. "You have a ton of powerful witches there."

"That's the problem. We all put our energy into helping Johnny create this concealment shield, so it's not a hostile spell. My magic is a part of it, so my magic doesn't recognize it as a threat to combat. Hard to explain, kid, but we'll figure it out. Tell me about my Cass."

Her Cass. My bestie finally found his better half and now...

I couldn't think about it.

I tried to keep my voice upbeat: "Well, we have a great plan."

"Don't fuck with me, Evie. That's my soulmate in there. Give it to me straight."

My voice shook. "He's gone, T. Cho sent out some initial feelers but nothing came back. The sirens have him and no one can go in after him without the gate ripping them in half, according to my father at least."

I wasn't prepared for the wail that came through the other end of the phone. It was a cry of anger and desperation, coming from one of the strongest witches I'd ever met.

"But we have a plan," I hastened to add. "We're going to jump in a helicopter and fly to see the selkies. I'm going to convince them to go in after Cass and save him or something brilliant. Don't worry."

Silence.

Until finally, "The selkies...?" Her voice was airy on the other line. "The Selkies!" she shouted, making me jump.

"Yeah..."

"Evie. The selkies aren't shifters. Their ability to change forms is confined to their seal skins. Legend says that anyone with magical blood wearing a seal skin can become a selkie, even if only temporarily. Men and women used to try to steal the skins in order to harness their powers."

What was she suggesting? "Could I do this? Could

Brock and I temporarily become selkies enough to convince the underworld that we have a demonic energy signature?" It was as bananas as it got, but it was also the only plan we had that didn't rely on an untrained bartender.

"Yes," Tianna confirmed. "You and Brock could cloak your energy in demon magic to cross into the underworld and save Cass. At least, that's the theory."

Oh fuck. My alpha was not going to like this.

15 FRIEND OR FOE?

AFTER SUGGESTING I was crazy about twenty times, Brock finally agreed to at least ask the selkies if it was even possible to disguise ourselves as them. Now we were a few minutes away from their cove just off of the coast of Washington state. I'd always wanted to ride in a helicopter, just not like this.

"It's totally weird to me that the government knows exactly where we are right now." I reached out and rubbed the small lump on his shoulder, evident even beneath his t-shirt.

Brock grimaced. "If there's a murder within five miles of my location, I'll probably get blamed for it."

My eyes widened.

"I'm messing around," he told me before looking out at the open sea, but he was right. He'd taken a huge risk to protect his wolves.

Since we were on borrowed time, we'd convinced a fae pilot Brock knew to fly us to the selkies. I didn't want Cass in the underworld after nightfall.

"I'm going to do a water landing!" the pilot shouted over the sound of the whirring blades.

A *water landing?* That sounded scary, but his bird looked equipped for that sort of thing with floats for landing gear, so I just held on white-knuckled until he lowered us near the edge of the shoreline.

"I've got an inflatable boat," the pilot called out, and ten minutes later Brock had rowed us ashore.

"Let's be quick. Cass is … counting on us," I told Brock over the lump in my throat that had been lodged there since I found out the sirens had taken my bestie.

My alpha gripped my hand and we slow-jogged to the thick patch of forest where we'd seen the last selkie leader, or whatever she was.

Brock was staring into the forest. "Was it through here?"

"No, I think it was farther down." I pulled his hand and that's when the leader of the selkies emerged from the trees.

"Broke your sword again, kitsune?" the long-haired selkie asked behind black eyes that scared the shit out of me. Why couldn't they be beautiful mermaids instead?

I approached her, hands out. "Hey. We've got a situation and we're hoping you'll help…"

What would I offer her in exchange? Money? I doubted the selkies cared for that.

She raised an eyebrow. "Selkies don't help others. We stick with our own kind."

With that she turned her back and started to walk away.

What the fuck?

Rage boiled inside me.

"Fine! I'll fucking call the Akuma and sic them on your asses. I don't care. Meanwhile, the human Feds are locking up demons in concentration camps. I wonder how you and your group will fare in bunk beds on land!"

My chest heaved as the anger ripped through me. Brock stood there, wide-eyed, holding my hand tightly.

The selkie froze, then spun about, a demonic fire blazing in her eyes. "You dare threaten me?" The trees shook at her words, but I decided I'd gone too far to back down now.

"My best friend Cass, the little pink demon imp you met last time, was taken in the underworld, and I need to get him back. I'll threaten whomever I need to in order to make sure he doesn't die."

She sighed.

"Please, he's family." I whimpered.

Her face relaxed a little. "I wonder what it would be like to be that full of love for someone..." She sounded wistful, and I suddenly wondered if she had ever been in love.

I tried to hook the sale. "My witch friend said that if you loaned us two of your skins, we could—"

She gasped. "Loan you our skins? That's like asking someone to loan you their soul!" The fire was back in her eyes, burning more fiercely than before.

'We may have to call the pack. Take them by force,' I told Brock through our link. I wasn't taking no for an answer. I couldn't, not when this was our only chance at getting Cass back right now.

My alpha's eyes went wide and concerned, his mouth tight. War with the selkies wasn't exactly on today's agenda, I got that. But what else were we supposed to do?

141

Leaving Cass in the underworld as a prisoner of the sirens for a second longer than necessary was completely out of the question.

He dropped my hand and approached the selkie leader. "Times have changed. Supernaturals have become hunted overnight." Lifting his shirt, he showed her the small red bump on his shoulder. "I've been tagged like an animal, and now the government knows everywhere I go."

He allowed his words to linger until fear flickered in her eyes.

"It's only a matter of time before their witches find you and flush you out," I added for effect.

She crossed her arms. "So I let you borrow two skins, and what do I get? You're going to protect me from the humans?"

Brock shrugged. "Maybe. If you lend us two skins to cross over into the underworld, I, Brock Adams, will pledge an alliance with your clan. That means that if you're ever in need of protection or a favor, I'll grant it. No matter what."

Chills broke out on my arms. That sounded magically binding. A smile curled at the edges of the selkie's lips. "A favor and alliance with the alpha." She dragged the words out, seeming to ponder Brock's offer while stroking her stringy, long hair.

After a moment's pause, she snapped her fingers and two naked women walked out from the woods, a wet selkie skin draped over each of their arms in offering.

Thank you, Jesus!

I wanted to weep in relief, but kept my shit together. I could lose it on the helicopter ride back, but not here.

"I accept your offer, Brock Adams," the selkie leader said. She spat on her hand and held it out to him.

After a slight pause, he did the same, and they clasped hands. A small burst of magic, like a tiny shockwave, spread outward when their palms touched, and it was done. A magically bound contract.

Brock then turned to me. "Draping ourselves like this might hurt the baby. Cho has offered to go with me—"

"My skin would never hurt an innocent child," the naked selkie nearest me scolded Brock.

Her skin. She spoke about it like it truly was an extension of her soul.

Crazy.

"The baby will be fine," I told him. "I have to go. I have to be the one to get Cass."

Brock took one last lingering look at my belly and finally nodded, not bothering to hide his reluctance.

The selkie leader smiled. "It's all set, then. We'll lend you these two skins, and the moment you return from the underworld, you'll have them sent back here."

Brock nodded. "You have my word."

The girl nearest me grabbed the edges of the skin and shook it out, like a cloak. "Ready?"

My eyes widened. "Oh. Now?"

The girl nodded. "My skin must know that you do this with my permission. Otherwise it will kill you."

Brock made a strangled noise in his throat. "You said it wouldn't hurt them."

She snapped her head in his direction. "It won't as long as we do it my way."

"It's fine," I told them both, and bowed my head.

One second I was standing there, dry, and the next she

tossed this heavy, wet skin over my shoulders and I felt like I was floating in seawater. Like fully submerged.

"Good girl." The woman pet the skin, her fingers trailing along my back as if she were petting me. It's like the skin and I were one and we were floating in the ocean. There was also something dark there, lurking at the edges, probably whatever made it demon in nature, but I chose not to focus on that. Cass was a demon and there wasn't a dark bone in his body, so this could be okay too.

"Be good. I will see you soon," the selkie cooed in my ear, and I tried not to shiver. The seal's head was draped over my skull like a hood. I had no doubt it was terrifying to look at.

Glancing over, I saw that Brock was also wearing his selkie suit, a naked female stroking his back while she whispered in his ear.

Could this day get any stranger? We looked like we were about to start filming some weird porno.

"Now go, and don't forget to bring the skins back," the leader warned. "If you don't show, we'll pay a little visit to your pack."

Brock nodded. "We'll show. Thank you."

One of the females pointed to the skins. "You can take them off and on now at will. They will behave. But leave them on the entire time you're in the underworld unless you want to burn alive."

Oh God. I had to fight three sirens with this thing on?
Great.

With that, Brock and I turned and started to walk to the helicopter.

"Are we seriously doing this? Going to the underworld

144

looking like selkies?" Brock asked as the skins floated around us.

I stopped and faced him. "Look, I know you didn't sign up for this level of crazy. I totally understand if you—" He cut me off with a kiss to the lips.

"It was a rhetorical question, my love. Where you go, I go."

I couldn't help the smile that spread across my face as we headed home to walk through the gate to the under-world and save my best friend from psychotic sirens.

16 DIE, DEMON SCUM!

THE SECOND THE helicopter touched down in Eugene, Brock reached out through the pack link to bring Ray up to speed, and I whipped out my cell phone to call Tianna. By the time I disconnected the call, Brock was already directing an expectant look my way while he threw his waiting truck into drive. With the selkie seal skins in the back seat, he tore off the tarmac as if we had a date with the devil himself—which wasn't all that far from the truth.

"They haven't made much progress with Johnny's spell," I groaned, flinging my head against the seat-back in frustration. "There's no way Tianna will be able to help us out. She's freaking out about being stuck at Cottage Grove when Cass needs her." I closed my eyes to process all the feels. If Brock were in trouble and I couldn't get to him, I'd be losing my damn mind too.

"I'm sure she won't stop trying until she breaks through Johnny's spell," Brock said. "Ray is gathering our strongest wolves. I'm going to station them around the gate."

"Just in case another nasty creature tries to come out of it?"

"Basically, yeah. Besides, I'll feel better knowing they're there in case we need help."

"We're going into the fucking underworld, home of the Akuma and all sorts of other fun-loving demons. What could possibly go wrong?" I grimaced.

"We've got this," he said. Though he had no way to know how things would go, I appreciated the sentiment. The odds were stacked so overwhelmingly against us that I didn't want to stop to think about it. No matter what, I was going down there. I'd do anything for Cass.

"But if things get too dangerous down there, you come back here for help, and I'll get Cass out," he added.

I nodded, though I'd never leave him behind.

"We have to hurry. I can't shake the feeling that we're running out of time," I said, and Brock pressed the pedal to the metal; the dense greenery of Oregon whizzed by.

By the time Brock barreled down the driveway to our house, a couple dozen werewolves, my dad, and Cho were outside waiting for us. We threw our doors open, grabbed our borrowed selkie skins, wrapping them around us, and leapt out.

Right away, Sabine was in front of me. "How are you feeling?" she asked, staring deep into my eyes as if she were a medical instrument, trying to take my emotional temperature.

"Like I'm gonna kill some siren bitches."

"I see." She blinked at me a few times, but she couldn't quite keep the smile from showing on her face.

"The baby's fine," I told her, trying to hurry this up. "She's kicking up a storm. And I feel well too." I tried to move past her, but she stopped me with a gentle hand to the shoulder.

"You have to at least take a minute to drink and eat something. You're heading into the underworld, there's no telling what will happen once you enter." Her eyes were serious as she pressed a bottle of water into my hand and slung a backpack, presumably full of snacks, over my shoulder.

Shit, she was right. I needed to at least hydrate. "Thanks, Sabine. I'll do it while we move."

She hesitated, her eyes clouded with worry, but finally conceded. "I've filled the bag with your prenatal vitamins, electrolyte water, beef jerky, and dried fruits."

Chortling, I nodded. "Thank you." I was hungry enough to eat a whole pizza. Hell, several pizzas.

Adjusting the bag around my Glock and katana, I started walking toward the gate when Cho jogged up to me. "Evie, wait."

I turned to face her as she pressed Cass' iridescent, sequined booty shorts into my hand. I looked down at them, tearing up. Damn pregnancy hormones. They were the shorts he wore when he wanted to impress.

"What are these for?" I whispered around my mess of emotions.

"I cast a spell on them. The shorts will lead you to their owner. Once you're through the gate, just pay attention to their directions, and you'll find Cass."

Wow. I prayed I would one day be half the witch that these badass women in my life were. Between Cho,

Tianna, and Willemena, I had some serious catching up to do.

I squeezed her hand. "Thanks, Cho. This will help a lot."

"Don't worry," she said, squeezing back. "You'll find him."

I nodded a little too fervently, working to convince myself. Cass was family. I was getting him back. Without a doubt.

"I also don't figure it'll be all that easy for you and Brock to fight with those selkie skins hanging off of you. I have a spell that should work to mold them to your own skin so they don't slide off. We don't want to risk the underworld figuring out you aren't demons while you're down there."

No, we sure as hell didn't.

"That'd be great, thanks. What do you need us to do?" I asked, arranging the seal skin to fit a bit better around my shoulders.

"Nothing. Just give me a few moments. Oh and I'll remove the spell that keeps you from shifting. Just in case," Cho said, bowing her head.

Man, what would I do without this amazing witch? It was a smart thing to do since I might need to be in my fox form down there.

I nodded, calling for Brock. He stood next to me while Cho did her miracle magic, chanting once more in rapid-fire Japanese. By the time she'd finished, even when I twirled the selkie skin didn't budge. It had become light-weight like parachute material, and clung to me like a second skin.

I grinned. "Awesome, thanks."

"You're most welcome," Cho said.

Once more, I reached for her hand and met her eyes. "Thanks for taking care of my dad as well."

She turned to gaze at him and smiled. "It's my pleasure. He and I have been through a lot together. He's a good friend."

"Ready?" Brock asked me, taking one proffered handgun after another from Ray and slipping them into holsters strapped across his chest, hips, back, and thighs.

"Yep," I said, admiring his arsenal.

He looked up and grinned. "You're jealous of my guns?"

"So jealous."

"If you're a good girl, maybe I'll get you a few extra of your own." His grin was pure sinful mischief.

I winked. "As long as I don't have to behave too much."

Brock finished strapping guns to himself and we took off for the gate. Continuing our flirty banter was the only thing keeping me sane right now.

A dozen werewolves, a powerful witch, and a former kitsune trailed in our wake. Even with all of them as backup, we were nowhere near ready for what might hit us once we entered the gate. Still, I couldn't think about that now. All I could think of was Cass.

With the construction flag still in place marking the crack to the gate, Brock turned to me, taking both my hands. "You ready?" he asked.

To enter the underworld? The birthplace of all demons? *Hell to the no.*

"Yes," I said with a deranged sort of smile.

"That's my girl," he laughed, then immediately turned somber. "Promise me, no matter what happens, you'll take care of yourself and the baby first."

"Of course," I answered right away.

"Even if it means leaving me behind. Even if it means leaving Cass." His amber eyes were dead serious, and my heart skipped a beat.

Uh, fuck no, I wasn't leaving either of them behind.

"I mean it, Evie," he pressed. "If it's a choice between you and the baby, or Cass and me, you haul ass and get the two of you out."

Yeah … no. But I couldn't tell Brock that.

I didn't want to lie so I just nodded.

As I turned toward the gate, he gently grabbed my arm and turned me back toward him. "Promise me. You and our baby mean more to me than my life."

My heart thudded.

"I need to know that you'll be safe no matter what happens," he continued. "Promise me you'll leave me behind if you have to. Please."

Fuck, he knew me too well.

Staring into his eyes, I knew there was no way I'd ever be able to do that. He must have read it in my face.

"I need this, Evie. I need to know you'll survive this."

"Fine," I snapped, and he sighed in relief, the stray strands of dark hair across his forehead wafting upward. I leaned forward to whisper in his ear. "But you'd better make sure your fine ass ends up back here with me. I plan on making you my husband."

He smiled broadly, but concern clouded his usually brilliant eyes.

We clasped each other's hands and offered our friends

tight smiles that weren't returned. Every single one of them were freaked the hell out that we were about to enter the underworld—voluntarily.

"We're coming for you, Cass," I declared, and dove feet-first into the opening of the gate.

17 NO ONE FUCKS WITH MY BESTIE AND LIVES

AS BROCK and I stepped through the crack in the gate, a heavy, oppressive heat wafted up from the hard rock of the cliff we stood on, clamoring against my lungs. Resisting the urge to claw away the invasive heat, I tried to make sense of my surroundings, but didn't manage to make out much. It was so dark!

Pivoting, I slipped and started to slide down. I caught myself on the ledge and pushed myself back up. With a groan, I turned in search of Brock. We were on a fucking cliff.

"Ah," I yelped, when I found him right behind me.

"Are you all right?" he barked urgently, running his hands up and down the sides of my arms. "Are you hurt?"

"I'm fine," I said with a hand to my heart to steady its frantic thumping.

He continued running his hands along me. "You're sure you're okay? You almost fell!"

I did almost fall off a cliff in the underworld. That would have been bad.

"Totally." I patted my gun and katana to make sure they were in place after the drop. I hadn't bothered with my badge. It wasn't like underworlders would respect my authority. Down here, power trumped all, and power was determined by physical and magical strength.

"Okay," I said, looking around us in a circle. Though a faint orange glow illuminated our surroundings, it wasn't clear in which direction we should head. Small campfires glowed in the faraway distance, and a magical-looking light red haze colored the sky, but that was it.

"Let's make our way down this small cliff first," I suggested.

Brock nodded, and after about two minutes of treading carefully across rough ground, we were standing on the sandy floor of the underworld.

"Don't call out to Cass aloud," Brock cautioned me, even though I already sensed that wouldn't be a good idea. Though I couldn't see anyone, I also couldn't shake the feeling that we were being watched, and I had no desire to draw attention to us.

'Cass?' I tried through our mental link, but even before silence drew out in reply, I knew he either couldn't hear me or he couldn't respond. Something was interfering with the telepathic connection Gran had set up between us.

Drawing Cass' sequined, iridescent booty shorts from the back pocket of my jeans, where they barely fit, I squeezed them in one of my hands and closed my eyes, paying attention to whatever sign they'd give me.

There!

It was slight, but there was an undeniable draw pulling me straight ahead.

"That way," I whispered to Brock, pointing with my head. I stuffed the booty shorts back in my pocket, swept my long hair into a ponytail, and steeled myself for whatever lay up ahead.

The landscape was the same in every direction: dark and bleak. Black lava stone surrounded us. A deep orange glow illuminated the rocks from below, suggesting that lava might actually run amid them. Sharp crags divided up the landscape, limiting our view in any one direction. Beyond the orange glow slashing macabre shadows, there was no other source of illumination.

"What a cheery landscape," Brock mumbled under his breath.

"Let's find Cass and get the hell out of here. I have a bad feeling about this place."

"You'd be crazy if you didn't." He brought a gentle hand to the small of my back and urged me forward, bringing either hand in close proximity of a weapon.

He had to be feeling it too, like there were eyes in the great walls of rock.

A bead of sweat trickled down my back, and I picked up the pace, following the pulsing of Cass' booty shorts forward. Dodging a few large boulders, I stopped to scout the area.

"Where is everyone?" I whispered to Brock. "This is home to every nasty creature of our nightmares. It shouldn't be so quiet."

"I know." Brock didn't meet my concerned gaze, and swept our surroundings without ceasing. "Something is definitely off. We should have run into something by now."

"Well, we wouldn't want to disappoint you," a voice I

knew all too well called down to us. Calista's voice bounced and echoed across the hard surfaces, enveloping me in her energy.

Oh fuck.

I shook the sensation off and whirled, looking for her.

"If you want us to attack you, we'll be happy to oblige," another voice taunted. Similar to Calista's, it had to belong to one of her sisters.

"Lots of us will be happy to oblige," a third voice sang out. Eerily alike to the other two, it had to be the third triplet. "You've captured far too many of us, *bounty hunter.*" The siren spit out my title like it was as foul as this place.

Ah! There. I pinned my attention on the crest of a nearby ridge. Silhouetted by orange stood three identical women. Their kelp-colored hair appeared black, undulating around them as if it were alive, though heat waves probably caused the effect. With their mouths turned into identical snarls, they appeared appropriately ferocious.

But they didn't scare me. I was going to kill all three of the bitches for taking my bestie.

Brock pressed his back against mine, watching the opposite direction so no one could sneak up on us.

"We're here for Cass," I shouted to the sirens. "Give him to us and we'll leave. We're not here to cause trouble."

Though I sure as hell would cause a whole shit ton of it if they didn't hand over Cass right this second.

"That's not how kidnappings work. We're the ones who ask for something, and you're going to give it to us," Calista declared, sounding all too fucking pleased with herself.

I growled, low and long. I was going to strangle Calista

with her own stupid green hair, and then I was going to kill her sisters. Twice.

"Cass isn't a bargaining chip," I ground out, my voice deadly, wrapping the fingers of one hand around the hilt of my katana.

Calista laughed, empty and echoing. "That's exactly what he is. And if you want to see him alive again, you're going to do exactly as I say."

Heat flushed through every part of my body, and it wasn't the lava. Pure fucking rage bubbled within me. I was going to tear the sirens limb from limb.

Brock brought a calming hand to my shoulder and called up to the sisters. "What do you want in exchange for Cass?" he asked, but his muscles were tight. Rage coiled through him as much as it did me; he was just better at the diplomatic role.

"Isn't it obvious?" Calista sang out.

No, you fucking crazy bitch, it isn't.

"We want your bounty hunter girlfriend to open the gate to the underworld all the way. If she does that, then we'll hand over her ugly friend."

Oh hell no. I breathed hard and heavy through my nostrils. No one called my pot-bellied, pink furry bestie "ugly."

It also hadn't occurred to me until that moment that the full force of the sirens' army couldn't come through to Earth; the gate was still magically barring their entry. Yes, the gate was open a bit, and some creatures had managed to slip through it, but if the gate continued to be the reason no more creatures were coming through, I needed to do everything in my power to keep the gate doing its job.

Opening my mouth to unleash every insult I could think of, Brock shook his head in caution, and I restrained myself—barely.

"Why don't you open the gate yourself?" Brock asked.

"Oh, don't worry, we will if you don't cooperate, but it's much easier if she does," Calista answered, anger tingeing every one of her words.

Water started to flow down the side of the cliff where the three sisters perched, and I found my rage growing hotter as I remembered them trying to drown me.

"And if she opens it?" Brock continued, when he obviously had to fucking know that there was no way in hell I would open the gate all the way. Just one fog demon had been enough to nearly bring down the entire town, and it had stopped at one town only because it'd just been getting started when we killed it.

"*When* she opens it, that will be our business, not yours," Calista snarled. "After that, our little transaction will be concluded." With that she ... floated ... down the waterfall she'd created and landed on the ground before us. Her sisters followed until all three were standing about thirty feet away.

Good. Come closer so I can kill you easier.

"You must know we can't let you unleash a bunch of demons on the Earth..." Brock growled, hand on the butt of one of his guns.

Because, duh. These siren triplets were seriously cray-cray if they believed for a second I'd let them unleash the contents of the underworld on humanity.

"We're not asking you to *let us* do anything," the second sister said, taking one step closer.

"We don't need your permission," the third sister parroted.

This was starting to feel like an ambush, and my rage was only burning hotter. Purple magic began to leak from my skin and swirl around me, like it had before in Brock's living room.

"It's the only way you're getting Cass back," Calista added, like it was a matter-of-fact truth, eyeing my purple magic curiously.

"Like hell it is," I growled, letting all of the anger that had been boiling within me snap out in the direction of the three sisters.

My magic slammed into them, knocking them on their asses, but I wasn't going to stop. Not until Cass was with me and the sirens had drawn their last breaths. My boss Mack would deal. No amount of bounty money was worth the danger the triplets posed to all of humanity. I pulled my gun and ran at the sisters, firing as I went.

Brock's sure footfalls pounded out behind me. He had my back; bullets flared from his gun as well. One of them struck the second sister in the abdomen.

"Stop or I'm going to kill Cass!" Calista shrieked from her place on the ground. My purple magic covered her like a blanket, but I didn't have time to be pleased with myself.

Even though I assumed she was bluffing, the words sent a chill rushing through my veins, cooling the sweat misting my skin in an instant. I skipped a step, stumbled on a rock, and nearly fell into a trickle of bright orange fire. Brock whipped a strong arm around my shoulders, heaving me back with a fierce pull. Then both Brock and I lowered our guns.

"You have to calm down," Brock implored. "I can't handle anything happening to you or our baby."

Bringing a hand protectively around the swell of my abdomen, I leaned into him while forcing myself to breathe slowly and deeply. He was right. I had to calm down.

We were in a standoff, and I was about to advance toward the sirens—fuck their threats about Cass—when my intuition nagged at me. The sirens were still trapped under my purple magical blanket, so I slipped Cass' booty shorts out of my back pocket, gripped them tightly again, and closed my eyes, secure in knowing that the siren sisters were still struggling to get out from under my magic.

My gut told me to head left instead of continuing on toward the sirens. Cho's spell, it had to be.

"We go left," I whispered to Brock, who didn't question me.

"Halt!" the third siren called out. I glanced back to see them frantically trying to help their wounded sister and peel back the layers of my spell.

Hah. Maybe I was a decent witch after all.

But when neither Brock nor I answered, the sirens were left mumbling among themselves, obviously thrown off that we were on Cass' trail. The next time I turned around, they were no longer at the base of the outcropping of rock. *Weird*. I figured they were trying to catch up to us or cut us off. *Damn*. Either wasn't a great option before we secured Cass. After that, they could bring it on, because I was going to mow every one of them down.

Jumping across black rocks like we were running through a dry riverbed, we arrived at an open clearing.

There was no clear path forward, and so I stopped and focused on Cass' little shorts again. Only this time they urged me the opposite way, in the direction we'd just come from.

"What's wrong?" Brock asked.

"Cho's spell is now saying that way." I signaled with my head. "Do you think they're moving him?"

"They must be." But when we trailed our gazes across the underground lava pit, we saw no signs of movement. We didn't even spot the sirens, though I was pretty sure they must be moving toward us.

My gut churned with unease, and I called to Cass through our telepathic link again. Still crickets. "I don't like this," I told Brock, who pursed his lips and took a step closer to me.

"What's to like?"

"I feel like they're messing with us," I said.

"I just shot one of them and you trapped them in a blanket of magic. They're definitely messing with us," he affirmed.

"I'm not sure we should follow Cho's spell anymore." Though how else were we going to find Cass if we didn't follow his magical booty shorts? But I couldn't shake the feeling that something was really wrong.

"Then we don't." Brock didn't even question my instincts. "In which direction do you think we should head?"

Taking a few moments, I tuned in to our surroundings. The heat had regained its oppressiveness—think the middle of the summer in humid Alabama times two, and all that beneath a heavy, dense seal skin meant to insulate from cold water temperatures. But even amid the sweltering heat, a chill tickled at the edge of my senses. Was it Cass trying to reach me through our link? Was it my intuition again?

Like a swift punch to the gut, I realized what it was.

"Someone's trying to cast a spell over us," I said to Brock so softly that he had to crane his head forward to make out the words. But when he did, his eyes widened, and he pulled me into his arms, holding me in a tight embrace while he whispered in my ear.

"Can you tell who or what it is?" he breathed.

I shook my head.

"Can you cast a spell to protect us?"

I shook my head again.

Wait, I could do one of those protection bubbles Tianna taught me to create, though I had no idea if it'd be strong enough to hold. After all, we were in the *underworld*, for fuck's sake. This was the birthplace of the scariest magic in existence, along with the most frightening of all monsters to wield that power.

"Whatever you just thought of, do it," Brock urged, and I didn't waste time. Whatever magic was being cast our way was far enough along for me to feel it amid the distraction of lava spurting all around us.

I squeezed Brock in my hold and closed my eyes. Right away, I pictured my energy, my magic, as a bright light that I could extend out of myself. When the white glow was bright within my mind's eye, I directed it over Brock and me, draping each one of us individually in its protection. When I was satisfied that the light fully coated Brock and me from top to bottom, I whispered so softly that I wasn't sure even Brock could hear me, and he was literally pressed against me...

"My light, my magic, infinite energy of the universe:

Protect our physical bodies from all harm.

Repel any and all attacks from the forces of darkness.

While we remain within the underworld, keep us healthy, strong, and safe."

Okay, so it was more like a prayer, but Tianna had said words contained power, and so I was giving it all I had.

I added, "And please help us kick some serious ass."

Brock's murmur of a chuckle was the only signal that he had heard my obviously made-up spell after all, but I still prayed it worked.

Releasing Brock, I allowed my instincts to guide me instead of Cass' booty shorts, which I now suspected had been magically tampered with. When my body pointed in the direction I'd last spotted the sirens, and I started in that direction, Brock grabbed my arm.

"Wait," he said. Pulling me back against him so no one could eavesdrop in this place where the rock itself seemed to watch us, he breathed, "Use your illusion power. Project out several of you."

"I'm not sure I can. I've only practiced it like twice."

"Third time's the charm," he urged.

I sighed. "They'll know I wouldn't leave your side."

"Then you'll have to."

I stared at him. He stared right back, apprehension at separating shimmering in his amber eyes. An orange glow reflected in them as I finally nodded. We needed every advantage we could get, however slight.

My dad had told me the secret to my illusion magic was to not think too hard on it. So before I could worry about how I'd accomplish it, I simply pictured three identical copies of myself, glowing bubble of light included, pushing some of my magic into the intention.

When I opened my eyes, nothing had happened. Like at all.

Shit. I guess when my dad meant don't think on it too hard, he actually meant to think on it at least a little.

Summoning more of my magic, feeling it filling the well inside my chest, I clenched my eyes again and envisioned three separate versions of myself. I pictured every detail about myself that I could, even going so far as to have the other me's smile confidently.

When the three images of me were fully concrete within my mind's eye, I directed every bit of the magic within myself toward them. Even when I started straining from the effort, I kept going, and only once the three other versions of me were fully enveloped in a cloud of my purple magic did I release it.

In a rush, the remainder of my magic slammed into the three versions of me, and my eyes popped open.

I startled when I spotted three exact copies of me circling us, but then a huge grin split my face. Brock stepped away from me and walked into the middle of the projections so as not to give away which Evie was real.

"You did it!" Brock whispered.

I nodded. "Pretty awesome, huh?"

"Hell. Yeah. Now let's get moving."

As Brock and I set off in the direction where we'd last seen the sirens, the three copies of me took three different paths. If we were lucky, one set of me would come across Cass. I couldn't exactly see through the eyes of my replicas, but I had the feeling that if one of the other me's saw

Cass, I'd know it—and then we'd haul ass to wherever he was.

We'd already been down here far too long. It was time to find Cass and end the sirens.

I moved faster across the rocks that made every one of our steps uneven, but I didn't run. Brock, Cass, baby, and I were getting out of here alive and well.

18 SIREN SOUP

BECAUSE THE BOOTY shorts had clearly been tampered with, we were going off my newly-trusted intuition instead, which I was hoping was a little bit of magic. I just felt in all my being that Cass was this way.

Once we got to the spot where the sirens had struggled, a mixture of water and blood still marring the ground, I took a left toward a sharp, jutting rock.

"Evie?" Brock asked one of my illusions. Either he was a good actor or he was confused about which one was really me.

I didn't answer. I didn't know if we were being watched and I wasn't sure I could make my illusions talk. We were headed right for the giant cliff, and my alpha was no doubt wondering why, when a crevasse appeared in the side.

'*Cass!*' I shouted through our bond, and this time I swore I felt something—a tugging at our connection.

Brock eyed the three-foot opening and pulled two guns, one for each hand, before slipping inside.

What the fuck? No word, no hesitation, he just dipped into the cave entrance like it was no big deal.

I scrambled to catch up, my illusions running with me. Could I leave one outside this opening like a sentinel? That sounded like some advanced level shit, but it was worth a try. Slipping into the small opening behind Brock, I attempted to leave one of my illusions outside while bringing two in with me. I had to focus on the projections of myself so that I wouldn't lose them or make them look spectral. Creating them was pretty easy, but keeping them solid was a challenge.

As we stepped into the darkness, the smell of sulfur and rotting sewage hit me hard. We'd walked right into a little side tunnel. There were two ways we could turn: left or right.

Come on, Cass, where are you?

My left hand went tingly and my eyes widened. Was I doing magic? Or did we have help? The tingling felt friendly, like something familiar I couldn't place. Without waiting, I turned left and dragged my two projections with me. Brock brought up the rear, the cocking of his shotgun ricocheting off the walls. He'd pulled out the big firepower.

We were on Cass' trail, I knew it.

Following the maze of cave tunnels, we were led to a bigger opening with another split, left or right.

Loud voices projected far below, and I placed my finger to my lips so Brock would know to keep quiet. As I inched closer to what seemed almost like a balcony with people below, I peeked over and quickly snapped my head back in.

Fucking mother fuck!

Two of the sirens were at the base of this huge cave, and spread out around them were over a thousand demons.

This shit was bad.

Like apocalyptic bad.

"Earth no longer trusts supernaturals!" Calista called out to the demons before her, arms out the side of her body as she projected her voice with strength.

The demons rose up in a mighty, angry cry, muffled with grunts of agreement.

My right hand tingled in warning, but I wanted to stay and hear what they had to say.

"Humanity is ripe for the taking!" the second sister cried out.

"It's now or never!" Calista yelled.

A wide-eyed Brock was standing before me; my right hand was tingling so much it was becoming painful. I recognized the magic signature then. My mentor, Tianna. It was her. She'd somehow broken free and was helping me!

"To the gate!" Calista cried, startling me from my realization. The cave started to shake as thousands of footfalls rattled the rock beneath us.

Oh fuck fuck fuck.

They were going to try to force it open.

I snapped to my feet and bolted to the right.

'Cass, you fucker! Where are you?'

We needed to get the hell out of here and get to the gate before they did.

'Ev!' His muffled voice barely came through. Tianna must have worked on whatever was blocking us.

A sob ripped through my throat when I heard that raspy smoker's voice.

'Cass! I'm coming!'

'Evie! You're here?' He sounded like he was talking through a pillow, muffled and far away, but it was better than nothing.

I ran blindly through the halls carved from the rock, trying to concentrate on my projections, which ran with me, along with the one I'd left outside the cave entrance, as well as Brock's footsteps behind me. When I rounded the corner, I caught a sliver of Cass' pink fur inside an open room.

'Don't come for me! It's a trap!' he screamed into my mind just as I ran into the room, gun drawn.

Thanks to my bounty hunter training, I took in the scene and started shooting. Cass was magically handcuffed to a metal ring that looked cemented into the rock wall. A large, ugly-ass demon was standing off to the right, talking to one of Calista's sisters. I got three bullets out before a wall of water slammed into me, knocking me backward into Brock.

Oh fuck that.

I'd never been so pissed in all my life. I screamed with rage and leapt into the wall of water. I was a fucking seal, right? I'd swim through this and rip that bitch's head off her body. My purple magic lashed out wildly as I broke through the wall of water and landed on the other side. Dripping wet, with a useless gun, I pulled my katana.

The siren bitch looked at me, her mouth gaping open in shock. She was holding her abdomen, which was bleeding freely. One of my bullets had found its mark.

But she wasn't staring at me. One of my illusions stood

next to me. That's what had her transfixed. Brock was roaring on the other side of the wall of water, but I had to push his panicked desperation away.

"Kill her!" the siren roared at the demon, who also looked like he'd taken a bullet.

The demon looked from me to my illusion, and deciding on my projection, leaped straight for it.

Bad idea.

With a battle cry, I surged forward and brought my katana down on the back of his neck, severing his meaty head in one clean slice. I'd never felt that powerful, like my magic was surging wildly through me and lending me super strength. It also felt a little dangerous, like I hadn't given it direction, and so it was capable of anything.

"You little meddlesome bitch!" the siren roared.

I sensed a thud at my back and was pleased to see Brock, in his wolf form but with the seal skin still attached. He'd probably used his alpha power to come through the water wall, and now we were going to kill this bitch once and for all.

'I'll carve her up, you take off her head,' I told him through our pack link.

Brock gave a wolfish grin.

Cass was silent, watching from his post on the wall. It looked like his cuffs kept him from doing magic; otherwise he'd be helping.

Brock and I stalked toward the siren and a grin spread across her lips as she built a water ball in her hands.

"Don't you know?" she cackled. "My sisters and I are some of the most powerful creatures in all the underworld. There's nothing you and your mutt can do to weaken us."

Pulling my magical shield over myself, because I knew she was about to throw that water ball at my face and try to drown me, I felt my projections pop out of existence. It was too hard to concentrate on them any longer anyway.

Holding my katana out before me, I stretched my purple magic along the blade. "Wanna bet?"

Taking in a deep breath, she blew on the ball in her hand. It flew across the room with lightning speed, covering Brock's entire wolf muzzle in water.

Oh damn! The protection I'd placed over Brock earlier seemed to have fizzled out along with my projections.

When she threw another water ball at Cass, I snapped back into motion.

Instead of freaking out, like the siren no doubt expected me to, and like I really wanted to, I charged forward with my father's sword, so much rage coursing through my veins I thought it might consume me.

The next water ball came right for me ... but I was ready. It disintegrated as it hit my shield and splashed across my face. A purplish blast of magic shot from the tip of my sword and wrapped around her throat like a rope. The panic in her eyes brought me the satisfaction I had been searching for since these sirens started wreaking havoc on Earth.

I needed to end her quickly so I could help Brock and Cass. While my purple magic choked her, she threw water around the room wildly. In an expert maneuver that would have made Haru and Reo happy, I cut across her abdomen with one slash.

Blood, mixed with water, gushed from her stomach, and I wasted no time in bringing my elbow up to clip her in the chin. She threw her head backward and exposed her throat.

Kill shot.

Bringing my katana up, I cut into her neck with every ounce of strength I had. I wasn't prepared for what happened next. Hissing steam erupted from her body as her head fell to the ground. Then murky red water gushed from her neck like a waterfall, pooling around her body.

What. The. Fuck?

'Evie!' My gaze flicked over to see Cass was drowning. The water ball that the siren had thrown had consumed his entire head. Brock seemed to have used his alpha magic to expel his water bubble and was chewing at Cass' cuffs, to no avail. They had to be magically protected or Brock's canines should have caused some damage.

'*The seal skin saved me,*' Brock told me hurriedly. Ahh, so that was it.

Without thinking, I burst forward and built up purple magic in my palms. I tried to shape it, intending to somehow counteract the water ball, but it just sort of built into a flat pancake. Fuck, it would have to be good enough. When I reached my bestie, I threw it over his mouth and waited. Red-tinged water was rising rapidly in the small cavern, already at my ankles, and I wondered what kind of shit I'd just unleashed by killing one of the famous siren sisters. The hissing releasing from her neck got louder. I worried she was going to blow like some water bomb.

Cass coughed, spitting the water out and gasping for air, my purple magic finally helping him breathe.

Thank God.

"Cass!" I whimpered, clinging awkwardly to him as he

was still pinned to the wall.

"You shouldn't have come for me," he whimpered.

Nonsense. "You know that's impossible."

Brock urged me to stay on task: *The gate. We gotta get out of here. I can't break his chains.*

Right. The demon army was marching for the gate, and I was pretty sure the other two sirens would have felt the death of their sister. The water was up to my knees. Being underground in a cave filling with water had my lungs hiccupping with panic. I grabbed the chain pinning Cass to the wall and flooded it with my purple-hued magic.

Nothing happened.

Cass yanked in vain against the chains that bound him. "Just go! I'll figure it out."

"Nobody is going anywhere!" I shouted.

Evie, you promised, Brock said in my head. *The baby.*

I growled. *I fucking lied, okay?*

Cass was my family. I had to figure this out. Like hell I was going to leave Brock behind to deal with who knew what might pop up next.

I rubbed my face in anxiety.

Think.

How do I break magical cuffs when I'm a shit magic user? *Think, think, think.*

Then it hit me. I didn't have to break the cuffs. I could let Tianna or Cho do that. I just needed to disconnect them from the wall.

Leveraging my foot against the wall, I slid my katana into the opening between the chains of the cuffs and the ring that held them in place.

Please don't fucking break my sword. That was literally

the last thing I needed right then.

With every ounce of strength I could muster, I pulled down on my sword with all my weight. A snap rang throughout the cave and I nearly cried in relief. It was just barely audible above the hissing dead siren about to explode.

"Let's go!" I shouted.

I knelt in front of Cass and he leapt onto my back. No way would my vertically-challenged bestie be able to walk or fly his way out of here; there was too much water. I was going to have to piggyback him like we did in boot camp at the academy.

Brock waded through the water, which was nearly up to his neck on all fours, and took a right, back down the way we'd come. Holy shit, this entire place was filling up with water, and fast. How?

'You killed a siren!' Cass mind-messaged me. His voice was clearer than it had been before, though still not what it used to be.

'I did.' I was still stunned I'd done that. *'Brock shot another one of them too, but with our luck, she's still kicking.'*

"How's T?" he asked.

"She's fine." I had no idea if she was still with the Blacks, stuck on their land, but I didn't think so. Not with the magical help I'd been feeling since we'd gotten here, and I didn't want my bestie to worry.

Brock followed on my heels as I weaved in and out of the winding halls of rock, but it still wasn't fast enough. There was too much water, and it was flooding us from all directions.

Then Brock made a hard right and I saw the water was flowing out of a hole in the side of the mountain. The same one we'd come through earlier on our way to get Cass.

The moment I stepped back out beneath the dark underworld sky, a startled scream lodged in my throat.

"My sister!" Calista shrieked somewhere up above us on the cliff face, water pouring down its steep side like a raging waterfall.

Oops. She was majorly pissed.

Brock shifted quickly into his human form, throwing on shorts from my pack, and turned to face me. "Evie, the demons will be making their way down to this valley any second. From there they'll head straight up to the gate."

There were two cliffs and a valley of lava rock between them. We needed to get across the valley and up the next cliff to where the gate sat before the demons did.

I nodded to Brock. "I got this. You take Cass."

He frowned.

"Take him! We don't have time!" I snapped.

Brock pulled Cass off of me and slung him on his hip like you would a toddler. At another time, the image would have made me crack a smile.

Taking in a deep breath, I pushed my awareness out, and with it my projection power. Over twenty Evies popped out beside me and in front of me.

I looked at Cass and Brock, their eyes wide. "Run!" I barked.

With that we took off like our asses were on fire. A line of twenty Evies followed us, racing across the lava rock-filled valley, hoping to reach the cliff that the gate was perched on before Calista could drown our asses.

"KITSUNE!" Calista roared, and it started to rain. The dark, dense sky above us shed fat droplets of water.

A quick, tiny peek over my shoulder and I nearly pissed myself. Hundreds of demons were descending from the top of the rock, spilling out onto the open valley —right on our tail.

Calista thrust her arm out and lightning struck from the sky and zapped one of my projections, making it disappear in an instant.

Fuck. That was efficient. Nineteen more to go.

I'd never run so fast in all my life. Brock was right next to me, half naked, with a seal skin draped across his back, carrying Cass.

When we got to the base of the rock cliff that held the gate at the top, Calista zapped another one of my projections. I could hear the footsteps of the demons they were so close, pounding a terrifying rhythm.

Without thinking, I scaled the wall like a fucking pro rock climber. I'd done some rock climbing at the academy but never without a harness and ropes. I grabbed handholds and footholds in a blind panic as Brock pushed my ass when I got stuck in parts. I had to make sure I didn't scrape by big-ass belly. I was way too pregnant to be doing this shit. Cass urged me on, and we made it. We fucking made it to the top! Thank God the climb wasn't fully vertical or there was no way I could have managed it.

Wasting no time, I leapt through the crack where I could see the trees of our property in Oregon.

Home sweet home.

"So nice of you to finally join us," a male voice called over my shoulder, and I swallowed hard.

Turning slowly, my gaze landed on three Akuma, one of them holding a knife to my father's throat.

Oh fuck. Take me back to the underworld.

19 AKUMA DOUCHEBAGS

"DROP the knife and back away from my dad," I snarled, drawing my katana, sensing Brock climbing out of the gate behind me with Cass on his back a few moments later.

The Akuma demon threatening my dad only sneered, its ugly black teeth on full display. "Not until you open the gate to let our demon army through." He ran a gray tongue across sharp teeth, and bent further over my dad in his wheelchair, pressing the black blade against my dad's throat until he drew a few droplets of blood.

I squeezed the hilt of my sword, working to remain calm. There was no way in hell I was going to let anything happen to my dad, especially not now that I finally had a chance at a life with him in it. But I also wasn't opening that damn gate.

I edged farther away from the gate, closing the distance between me and the fucker threatening my dad. There was no easy move here. The three Akuma were much like the ones who had tried to kill me at the selkie cave. They looked almost like humans, if said humans were strung out on pure evil. The two men and one woman were hulked out, bulging muscles straining through minimal clothing. What looked like black sludge circulated through their veins, visible just beneath the surface of their flesh. But the worst thing about them were their eyes. This particular set of demons had black, pupil-less eyes, rimmed in red; dirty, black, stringy hair framed them.

The other two demons threatened Cho and Tianna. Each held a similar obsidian blade pressed to the witches' throats. Neither woman appeared afraid, but rather biding their time for the opportunity to rip the fucking Akumas' throats out. Even the composed Cho revealed murder in her gaze.

The Akuma threatening my dad bent his face closer to him, but his stare remained on me as he spoke. "Open the gate, kitsune, and we'll let all of you go."

There was no chance they would. The Akuma weren't the kind of snuggly demons to leave survivors behind. Besides, I was going to kill every single one of them for coming here and threatening the people I loved. My patience was at an all-time low. We'd only just managed to recover Cass, only to return to this...

"T," Cass whispered, edging around me, his gaze jumping across all of the threats.

Tianna's eyes brimmed with emotion as she took in her little pink lover. This should have been a happy reunion. The fae-witch smiled at Cass, and my bestie took another measured step toward her. Like me, he was moving into position to take the Akuma down.

"Don't fucking take another step," the Akuma seethed.

Oops. Guess we weren't being very sneaky.

Brock was poised to move in the opposite direction as Cass, but now he froze, broadcasting through my mind, making an announcement to the entire pack: *'Wolves, we have a situation. Three demons are on pack land, and two very pissed-off sirens will be trying to make their way through the gate to us any minute now, a demon army right behind them. I need all hands on deck. Wherever you are, whatever you're doing, head to the gate immediately.'*

Had I not been able to hear him, I wouldn't have realized he was communicating. A few moments later, Brock spoke just to me. *'Ray is getting Haru, Reo, and Molly. We'll have more than a hundred wolves to back us up in minutes.'*

I didn't reply in any way. Brock didn't even look at me, his eyes pinned on the Akuma. Some of the more intelligent of demons, it was better for them not to get overly suspicious. If we moved fast, maybe we'd have the chance to take them out before they could hurt my dad.

I had no doubt Calista was on her way. If the bartender demon had managed to walk out of the underworld without a problem, the gate wouldn't keep her out. She'd slither her way through the crack, and she'd bring her scary-ass sister with her, even if the other siren was wounded.

Calista had been bad enough before. Now that I'd killed one of them, and Brock had shot the other one, she was worse. She was going to be a pain in my ass until I lopped her head off too.

'Let's kill these assholes before they hurt my dad and the sirens can get up here,' I said to Cass, and then Brock.

"Open. The. Gate," the Akuma growled a final time, pulling the blade tighter against my dad's throat. A small rivulet of blood rolled down his neck and I swallowed hard.

"Okay, okay. I'll do it," I lied, half holstering my katana and placing my hands palms up. "I need to connect with the earth," I told him. Bending down, I placed my palms over the earth and tried like hell to come up with a plan. I didn't know how to open or close that damn gate, but my dad's life depended on it.

My dad was the only one without some sort of supernatural powers, and he was the only one bound to a wheelchair. Cho and Tianna looked ready to tear their captors limb from limb the first chance they got, and I was pretty sure Cho was hoping to punish the Akuma hunched over my dad.

But the blade was too firmly pressed against my dad's throat. And the witches had no leeway either.

We needed a distraction, and if there was anyone who was good at distracting, it was Cass. With his hot-pink fur and sparkling personality, there was no one better.

'Cass,' I mind-messaged. *'I need a big distraction. Can you handle that with the cuffs still on?'*

'Oh I can definitely handle it. I'm going to strangle that nasty demon for daring to touch my woman.'

'Brock,' I said. *'Cass is going to distract them. Be ready to move in.'*

Brock cracked his neck, the fingers of both his hands wiggling, ready to grab the guns at his sides. He could have them drawn, aimed, and shot in seconds.

'Ready?' Cass asked me.

'Go for it.'

And go for it Cass did. I wasn't sure what I'd been expecting since I hadn't really thought things through. But if I had thought of it, I'd probably have pictured Cass using his illusion magic to project a threatening monster or something. He didn't have his hoverboard, so he couldn't zip around them to distract, and with his hands bound maybe his magic was limited—his signature red magic balls all originated in his palms.

Regardless, I hadn't expected what he actually did, and I was pretty sure I could say the same for every single person and creature gathered in the clearing next to the gate to the underworld. As one, we all stared at my furry best friend, whose cuffed hands were above his head while he undulated his entire body side to side. He started to hum his own music while wiggling his hips to the beat. With his shiny gold Speedos in place, it was hard to miss any of his movements.

"Badum, badum, badum," he sang, eyes closed as he danced to the beat of his own drum, stepping into full view of the Akuma. He flicked his pelvis forward a few times in moves that would have made Michael Jackson proud, circling his hips while he did a slow turn for his captive audience.

Cass made his hot pink fur, potbelly, horns, and tiny wings work to the max for him as he gyrated.

'W-what is he doing?' Brock spluttered into my head.

'Isn't it obvious? He's distracting.' The only problem was that I'd also let him distract me.

Shaking every part of his body at once, he really got into his groove, humming even louder, working his booty like he was born for the role. He was moving like a tiny demon imp stripper, and for the first time I was glad that his hands were bound. If not, he might have taken his task of distraction to levels none of us but Tianna were ready for.

"What the hell?" The Akuma holding my dad watched my bestie in horror, his knife hand slackening as the shock of seeing a random stripper imp settled into him.

"Baboom," Cass sang, and rocketed his hips in one direction, shiny gold blazing the way.

I burst from the ground and whipped my sword the rest of the way from its holster and up in one smooth motion, lunging at the Akuma threatening my dad. The demon spun his head in my direction, but by then I'd skewered him straight through the side. I wrenched my katana free from his abdomen, and while the Akuma gasped in pain, his eyes blazing fury, Brock shot him straight through the head just as he was moving to bring the blade across my dad's throat.

One quick glance over my shoulder told me that Tianna and Cho had managed to deflect the hold their captors had over them as well. Both women now faced off with an Akuma, the demons palming their obsidian blades that no longer posed much of a threat.

Cass ceased his dancing and ran to my side.

"I'm okay," I said quickly. "Go help Tianna." Not that Tianna looked like she needed the help. The Amazonian fae-witch was angrier than I'd ever seen her; even the Akuma seemed nervous as he sized her up.

"Go help Cho," I told Brock, though Cho's mouth was moving so fast that she'd have a kill spell ready in no time. Still, I had this demon under control.

Black blood dribbled from the side of his head as he lay weakly on the forest floor, dying.

A lopsided grin pulled at the corners of his mouth. "Blue ... harvest ... moon."

My eyes snapped to the sky, where a full moon glowed. *Oh. Fuck.*

I'd forgotten that Calista had been waiting until some special moon in order to be able to open the gate. This was that day. The day that she and her sisters would have the power to open it themselves. But it must be a challenge for them or they wouldn't have asked me to do it for them in order to release Cass. So maybe I had some time before they'd get it fully open without my help.

"An army of demons are on their way. You have doomed humanity," the dying Akuma commented coolly.

Like hell I had! I was done with this scumbag.

"I killed one of the triplets." It was my turn to grin. "And another one of them is sporting a gunshot wound to the gut." Pressing the blade of my katana against his throat, I pushed slightly.

His face faltered for a moment before returning to a smirk. "Doesn't matter. Calista can do it herself. She's"— he turned his head to the side and coughed—"powerful." He wheezed, black blood dripping from his mouth.

Enough of this shit. I needed to close that gate once and for all. I raised my sword.

"So am I."

Without hesitation, I roared a final time. With a swift downswing, the motherfucking demon's head rolled, black sludge oozing from his open neck, pooling onto the ground.

Immediately, I looked to my friends. Cass, Tianna, and Cho were already staring at me, wide-eyed. Even the calm Cho looked shaken, her gaze flicking back and forth to the little construction flag marking the gate. I looked to my dad; his mouth was pressed into a hard scowl and his warm, brown eyes spoke of defeat, though we were surrounded by our dead enemies.

"Now..." He shook his head, his dark shiny hair sliding across his crown. "Now we must prepare for the fight of our lives. We'll need all the help we can get to protect the gate and push the forces of the underworld back where they belong."

My dad sounded like he was ready to push every single demon back into the dark pit they came from with his own bare hands, wheelchair be damned.

As if on cue, the first of Brock's wolves started to arrive. Brock grabbed the first one he saw and pressed his selkie skin into the man's arms. Following his lead, I took mine off too and added it to the wolf's load.

"Take another wolf with you and go to the selkie cave in Washington," Brock ordered. "Return these to the selkie leader with my thanks. And tell her that the gate to the underworld is open, but we'll do everything we can—"

I stepped forward. "Tell her I'm going to close it."

The wolf and Brock both looked at me. I tipped my chin high.

Brock nodded. "Tell her Evie is going to close it, and we will report back to her soon with an update."

If I couldn't believe in myself, then who could? It was nice to know that Brock was on my side too.

The wolf's eyes grew large as saucers, but he nodded quickly, turned on his heel, and ran off, grabbing one of the wolves running by him. The two of them sprinted back toward the house and the cars.

Phew. At least we didn't have to worry about the selkies coming after us for not returning their skins right away.

Now all we had to worry about was the entirety of the underworld unleashing its evil on the world. And I was the only one alive who could stop this.

What. The. Fuck?

I swallowed loudly, bending to wipe the Akuma gunk from my blade before sheathing it. "I guess I'd better get to shifting. I need to have nine tails before I can close this gate."

"And we don't have a second to waste," my dad said, wheeling forward as if looking for a way to help.

Brock stepped forward and held out his hand. "You just shifted yesterday. Two shifts so close together could hurt the baby."

Sabine stepped out of nowhere. "He's right."

Fuck. I loved being pregnant, but it felt like a handicap sometimes. This was one of those times.

At some point I would need to let go of all this fear and just trust my intuition. My gut said that neither my body nor my magic would hurt the baby.

"The baby won't be hurt. You're all going to have to trust me on that," I told them, and started to undress.

"Evie!" Brock reached out a hand to stop me.

My violet eyes flicked up to meet his and suddenly we were locked in an epic staredown.

"Do you trust me?" I asked.

I could see the moment the confliction crossed my lover's face.

"We've got company!" Haru cried out from where he

stood near the gate. I had no idea when he'd arrived. Molly must be here too.

Brock finally nodded and released my arm.

A flash of light had me spinning toward Tianna. Cass held up his hands and wiggled them, now free of the cuffs.

"You shift, Ev," Cass said, making his way toward me, Tianna right next to him. "We'll prepare to kick some major ass."

"Kick some major ass? I'm in," Molly said, and I turned to see her smiling beneath her purple head of hair as she appeared between a bunch of wolves, Haru and Reo at her side. The Japanese warriors weren't smiling.

"What's that sound?" Haru and Reo asked at the same time, but before any of us could answer, a deafening roar wafted up from the underworld and through the gate.

I knew exactly what the sound was. The demon army was rallying to march on Earth ... and kill us all.

20 PEACE OUT, MOTHERFUCKERS

I STOOD there for a long moment, nervous for this final shift and the responsibility it would bring. *Nine-tailed kitsune, closing the gate*. This was a moment I'd been working toward for months.

"Evie! We can't hold them long," Brock shouted as he fired his shotgun.

Taking a deep breath, I pulled forward my kitsune magic and let the transformation wash over me. This wasn't like the other shifts. There was something extra powerful in this final one. The ground shook a little as I slammed down onto all fours. My muscles lengthened and pulled faster than usual, and a shockwave of purple snapped outward away from my body before it dissipated.

On all fours, I peered behind me and counted my tails one by one. Nine tails. I'd done it. I'd completed my final shift and was now a nine-tailed kitsune.

As I turned my head, I discovered what my new and final power was. I now had the ability to automatically know which direction I was facing. I was like a human compass, which was a good thing for a woman who'd always had a shitty sense of direction.

"Okay, Evie. Do you see the gate?" My father had wheeled right up to me and was hopefully going to direct me on how to close it.

I glanced up from where I stood and saw that the gate was slowly ... opening.

'It's opening!' I shouted to Cass.

He relayed the message to my father. Fucking Calista was doing some witchy shit and I needed to counteract it. NOW.

"Now shift back," my dad urged me.

What? I just went through all this to become an all-powerful, nine-tailed kitsune!

"Your power will remain with your human body," he assured me. "You need the katana to close the gate."

Wasting no time, I started to shift back.

Sounds of a scuffle seeped through the gate, and I knew I had little time to seal it before Calista, her sister, and an army of demons invaded Brock's land.

A woman once more, I slipped on the sundress Sabine handed me and grabbed my katana.

My father navigated his wheelchair over the forest floor, following me toward the commotion at the gate. "You should be able to see the gate in human form now."

I looked up. Sure enough, my father was right. I could see the gate to the underworld perfectly, and it was wide open. Calista and her sister stood in front of it. The sister wasn't as injured as I'd hoped; Brock's bullet appeared to have pierced her side instead of her gut.

Behind the sirens, demons crawled up the cliff-side to invade Earth. The green symbols on the gate were swirling now, in a fast, dizzying circle. Cho and Tianna held the front line, magically projecting a shield to keep the sirens from breaking through, but it wouldn't last. Already, cracks were forming around the edges of their protection, suggesting it would soon break.

"What do I do?" I screamed, hating feeling this helpless.

My father took a steadying breath, and I struggled to latch on to the sense of calm he was trying to project. "There are symbols on the front of the gate. One of the symbols is a lock, and the katana is the corresponding key. Now that you have all nine tails, you can place the katana in the lock. Before now, the power would have ripped you apart."

Oh great. Now he comes out with the truth bomb.

Stepping closer to the backside of the open gate, I studied it more carefully. "The locks are spinning like crazy," I called out. It was as if a bank vault had been opened, revealing the complicated wiring and bolts—if said bolts were twirling and flashing with bright green light.

"That's because of the sirens' magic. You need to try to slow them down." My father's voice was steady, but high-pitched in such a way that gave away his nervousness.

"I won't be able to hold them much longer!" Cho screamed.

"How the fuck do I slow them?" I shouted at my dad, all manners flying out the window.

"Use your kitsune magic and just grab the gate! Physically grab onto the symbols. It's magic, and you're magical. You have the control, daughter. Now just use it. Remember your power."

"Be careful," Brock warned.

God. I felt like I was cutting the wire to defuse a bomb! Without knowing which wire to cut. Shit!

Chaos erupted at the mouth of the gate. Figures blurred past me, streaks of long-haired green.

The sirens had broken through.

Cass, Molly, and the pack would have to hold them off while I worked to keep the demon army from scampering out onto Earth.

Remember your power, my dad had said.

"Gran, help me," I muttered, thrusting my arms out and grabbing onto the fast-spinning symbols of the gate. A sharp force jolted through my hands, traveled up my arms, and sliced down my back. I yelped and almost recoiled, but managed to hold on, gritting my teeth as I strained against the magic thrumming through the symbols. They were moving wildly while my hands passed right through them as if I were an insubstantial ghost.

Taking a deep breath and shaking off the electrifying sensation of the locks, I pulled my purple kitsune magic forward, allowing it to flow out along my arms and rest in my palms.

Stop already, you fucker! I cursed in my head, as I pumped my purple magic into the spinning symbols. They crashed against my hand, delivering a deep, vibrating pain with each hit, almost as if they were real, although they looked translucent and spectral.

"Feel the earth beneath your feet," my father said just behind my shoulder. "Feel the kitsune power, the power of all nine tails."

My wrists felt like they might snap in half, but the

spinning symbols of the gate were finally slowing, becoming legible rather than a green blur.

What I imagined were bodies crashed behind me, and water splashed at my feet. I flinched.

"Don't worry, Evie. We've got your back," Haru said.

I nodded.

Focus. Breathe.

Shutting out everything outside of me, I pulled, searching for that connection to my magic. Since the day my magic had manifested, it had frightened me a bit. I had a healthy fear of how much it might do if fully unleashed. I'd kept the full extent of my power at bay by only pulling on small parts of it at any given time.

Now I was going to open the floodgates to my magic. I'd need to bring forth the motherload if I was going to close this gate and thwart a war on Earth.

The moment I opened the dam holding back my magic, nausea barreled up my body before sheer power coursed through me, overwhelming the sensation. The baby kicked hard within my uterus; she must have felt it too. But no part of me could ever hurt her. I was sure of it; I trusted my body and its instincts.

With a battle cry, I thrust my hands into the spinning symbols, bleeding so much purple magic that the entire gate was now glowing brightly with the color. A crisp snap punctuated the forest, and the symbols stopped moving entirely.

"You've broken the sirens' spell. Close the gate!" Cho roared behind me.

I risked a glance around the gate. Two large, misshapen demons had just waltzed through it.

Now or never.

Picking up my katana, I inspected the circle of symbols, searching for any type of hole among them that might be a lock I could insert my sword into.

"Feel each one!" my father shouted. He sounded farther away than before. Had someone taken him? God, I hoped not, but I couldn't focus on him right now. I could only focus on finding this damn lock. Everyone was counting on me.

Running my fingers over each symbol, the tingle of ancient magic spread throughout my body as I caressed this centuries-old gate.

"Hurry, Evie!" Brock sounded like he was in pain, and that caused adrenaline to pump through my system like never before. My hands started shaking as I ran them over each symbol, touching, searching for a crevice or a crack where I could insert my katana.

The fucking gate had a lock in it this whole time! And my katana was the key? I could have tried to close the gate weeks ago!

Frustration washed over me as I scrambled to find the one symbol that contained a hole. I was about to give up and just turn around to help with the fight when I finally felt something. A divot in the edge of one of the symbols.

"I got it!" I shouted triumphantly, my pulse beating excitedly in my ears.

"Now to close the gate, stick your katana inside the lock and turn it," my father shouted. "Don't let go until it's completely shut and locked."

Easy peasy, baby. This motherfucking gate was about to be closed for business.

A bolt of purple fire flared along the blade of my katana. It was as if my weapon knew what we were about to do. Finding that groove again, I inserted my blade into it and the sword began to vibrate, hard.

Alarm swept through me, but I held firm, and pushed with all my might until the base of the katana slammed flush against the symbol. It was a wonky thing to look at. A gate, invisible to everyone but me, floating midair with my sword hanging out of it. But even weirder was the vibrating. It had spread to my entire body, and even the ground had begun to shake a little.

Maybe this wasn't so easy peasy.

"Close it!" my father shouted again, and a howl sounded in the night. Brock's howl. I had to hurry.

Pulsing every ounce of my strength into the handle of my katana, first I took two steps, forcing the gate closed, shoving against my sword, which was wedged in the lock. And then I took a third step.

The earth was definitely moving, as if an earthquake were rumbling across it. The amount of energy this gate was pushing off was tremendous, and I felt every little bit of it. It coursed through me like a live wire, but I somehow managed to hold on, just like my father instructed.

Finally, I had no more than six inches left to close to the gate when a female hand came up behind me and clamped over mine, yanking backward, trying to dislodge my weapon.

Calista.

I didn't have to look back to know. I could smell the saltwater and demon sulfur on her.

"Evie!" Cass shouted.

I didn't think. I just reacted. Keeping one hand on the hilt of my blade, I released the other and spun, wrapping it around her throat. The amount of power coursing through me made me feel like I was the fucking Hulk. I had the power to rip her head from her body one-handed, that's how much magic flowed through me in that moment.

"Your time is up, bitch," I seethed.

A streak of gray sailed through the air, and then Brock's wolf landed on her back, pushing her forward into me.

"No!" Calista stumbled, loosening her grip on my blade.

I used the momentum of her fall to sidestep and shove her head into the crack in the gate as she fell to her knees in front of me.

The bulk of Brock's wolf body clung to her back, his nails digging into her flesh, forcing her to remain on her knees. Her hands dug into the shaking earth while her head wedged into the six-inch gap I had left to close in the gate.

"Please! I'll go back. I'll—" Calista begged.

But I clutched the hilt of my katana with both hands and dug my heels into the ground, pushing that damn gate with every ounce of power at my disposal. Calista's plea cut off abruptly as the gate severed her head from her body in one clean slice.

Her head fell into the underworld and her body collapsed at my feet, blood draining from her neck.

Holy shit. I'd finally killed that bitch.

"It isn't over!" my father shouted. "Turn the sword and finish it before the power overtakes you."

The vibrating traveling through the lock to my sword, and up my arms, was insane. I wouldn't be able to hold on much longer. My arms felt like Jell-O, and the trees off in the distance were rustling so hard with the way the earth was shaking that I thought there was a very real chance they might fall over.

"Gran, give me strength," I called, knowing that if she could help me she would.

A gust of wind whipped past me, delivering the scent of sage, and I smiled. *Gran.*

With a final push and a cry, I wrenched my blade to the left, like pushing through cement.

I screamed, forcing myself to keeping going even though my arms were so weak I wanted desperately to let go. Electrical currents ripped through my body as the katana slowly turned the lock.

My arms were shaking like I was holding onto a jackhammer.

'Evie!' Brock cried out into my mind.

"Don't touch her or you'll die," my father warned Brock quickly, leaning forward in his wheelchair.

I was a mother now. I would need to be strong in the days to come, for myself and for my unborn child.

Fuck this gate. Fuck it hard.

With a final push, my katana slid the glowing, green lock into place.

The gate released a blast of power so intense that it nearly knocked me backward. I slid on my feet but managed not to fall.

The shaking finally ceased, but I felt like I was still moving for a moment.

"You did it," my father whispered. "You can let go now."

Pulling my katana free with weak and wobbly arms, I spun around.

Holy apocalypse.

Brock was standing right behind me, naked and covered in black demon blood. The forest floor was littered with bodies. Mostly demon bodies. But I noticed a wolf among them, and the other siren too. I worried that wolf might be Sabine or Ray.

I struggled not to panic as I rushed to count heads to make sure my friends were alive. Molly, Reo, Haru, Cass, Tianna, Cho, Ray, Sabine ... everyone was okay. I felt the loss of the one wolf through the pack bond and the deep sadness that came with it.

"I'm sorry." I told Brock, looking at the fallen wolf.

This fucking nightmare was finally over but it wasn't without causalities.

He nodded. "Jerome died with honor." Then he stepped forward. "The baby." Brock stepped up and placed a hand on my belly, which the baby promptly kicked.

We both smiled.

"He's a fighter," Brock told me.

I stood on my tip toes and kissed his lips. "She."

I really had no idea what gender the baby would be, but I liked going against him.

When I turned again, Reo and Haru were kneeling before me, heads bowed. "It's been a great honor to serve you, kitsune," Reo said.

Emotion clogged my throat again, and I dropped to my knees to be at their level. "The honor was mine. I'm just glad it's over."

Haru nodded. "At least until another gate pops open."

My eyes widened. I couldn't say anything for a few beats. "What?" I finally eked out.

"There are dozens of gates all around the world. It's your task to make sure they all stay closed." My father wheeled over to me and handed me a rolled parchment.

What the fuck? More gates? *Screw that.*

I collected the rolled paper. "What's this?"

"A map of the gates. Given to me by my father the day I sprouted my ninth tail. Keep an eye on the news. If there's an increase in major crime, indicating elevated demon activity, you'll know what to do."

'Damn. I was hoping this was the last and only time we'd have to do this,' Brock lamented through our link.

'Same. Still wanna marry me?' This was a lot to take in…

'Yes. Like yesterday.' Naked as the day he was born, he scooped me up into his arms and started to walk with me to the house.

"Uhh … thanks for all your help, everyone. We'll be back soon!" I shouted to his pack and our friends.

"I'm locking us in the house for a week. Sex. Food. Sleep. That's it," Brock huffed against my chest.

A peal of laughter bubbled through me, and I wove my fingers through his hair. "You're the best one night stand I ever had."

He looked up at me with smoky, amber eyes. "I better be the *only* one night stand you ever had."

I shrugged. "No comment."

A girl's gotta have her secrets…

EPILOGUE

"YOU'RE DOING SO GREAT, BABY," Brock cooed in my ear.

Another contraction racked my body and I screamed. "Fuck this. I feel *everything*!"

"Can't you give her anything to help with the pain?" Brock was up in Sabine's face, his wolf close to the surface.

Sabine shook her head. "It's too late for an epidural. She went into labor so fast. She's already dilated to ten centimeters and the baby is crowning. Come on, Evie! One more big push."

This fucking child had better treat me like a queen. She'd better never back talk, better eat all her vegetables without a fuss, and never forget a single Mother's Day.

"It feels like I'm shooting fireballs out of my vagina!" I roared as I started to push again.

Cass had fought with Brock to be in the delivery room and was now staring in obvious shock at my crotch. All blood drained from his face so that his skin was a pale, pasty gray around his hot pink fur.

"That's it! Keep pushing!" Sabine screamed as pressure and pain sliced open my pelvis unrelentingly. When I thought I couldn't bear a second more of it, the worst of the pain receded ... and Sabine held up a tiny little ... baby.

Holy shit. Tears blurred my vision as I instantly fell in love with this little bald screaming ball of skin.

My little crotch goblin was beautiful.

Sabine's hand was covering its sex organs. In the end, we'd decided to wait and be surprised.

I couldn't speak. Tears streamed down my face as I opened my arms, and Sabine wordlessly lay the baby on my chest. I looked down between the baby's legs and smiled.

"It's a boy," I told Brock, who bent over my shoulder, squeezing my arm in gentle support.

Tears lined his eyes, but now they spilled over his cheeks. "Told ya so." He winked and leaned forward to kiss my cheek.

I laughed. "That's exactly what I wanted to hear after giving birth to our child: I told you so."

Brock nuzzled his forehead into the baby's chest and my neck, rubbing his alpha scent all over us. When he looked up, he was beaming. "Let's have another."

I grinned. "Um, you gotta let a girl forget the pain of labor before you suggest another one."

My little family was now three, and it was the best damn day of my life.

A sob pulled my attention to my left, where Cass stood, tears rolling down his cheeks, spilling into his pink fur. "I'm an uncle. That little fucker is so cute. I'm a fucking uncle!" he shouted.

The entire room laughed at that.

I knew that there would be good days and there would be bad days, but they would be mostly good. I was still the guardian of all these gates to the underworld, but with family and friends like these, the good would always outweigh the bad.

One year later

With the support of our family and pack, Brock and I survived the first year of Caleb's life. After all the monsters I'd faced down, I figured raising a baby would be easy as pie in comparison. Well, I'd been dead wrong.

For much of the year I was too sleep deprived to remember I was a badass supernatural bounty hunter and kitsune-witch hybrid who'd managed to seal the gate to the underworld. The first year was a blur of sleepless nights, foul diapers, and leaky breasts, but enough warm-and-fuzzies to make up for all the discomforts.

But now that I'd weaned Caleb, and my body was back to being my own, and looking and feeling much as it used to, I was finally ready.

I rolled over in bed, staring at Brock as he slept, the soft light of morning filtering through cracks in the blinds. He peeked an eye open and pulled me against him, wrapping warm, strong arms around me.

"It's not time to wake up yet."

He'd been saying that pretty much every morning since Caleb had entered our lives, no matter what the time.

"What if I told you I'm ready?" I worked to keep the telltale excitement from my voice, anticipating his reaction.

Both eyes flew open and he stared at me for a few beats. "Are you telling me what I think you're telling me?"

I grinned. "Yep."

"Fuck. Finally!" One of his big hands slid across my waist to squeeze my butt. "I never thought I'd have to beg a woman to marry me."

"Well, in all fairness, I have been kind of busy raising our son."

"Excuses, excuses." He rolled his eyes, but his ruse wasn't convincing me. His enthusiasm was bleeding into everything he did.

With a quick kiss, he threw back the covers and shot out of bed, reaching for his phone on the chest of drawers. His fingers whipped across the keyboard before he looked at me again.

I arched an eyebrow at him. "What was that all about?"

"I told the team to set Operation Wedding into motion. They've been on standby for months, ever since you accepted my official proposal."

Brock had gone all out. He'd wined and dined me, showered me with flowers, and arranged dinner under the stars before getting down on one knee to pop the big question—officially. It was perfect.

"Operation Wedding?" I barked out a laugh. "Are you serious?"

"Hell yeah!" But he'd already turned around and was pulling clothes out of the dresser. I watched his fine ass slip into boxers with a lamenting sigh. Despite the new baby, I'd still managed to get my fill of the man; I didn't think I could ever grow tired of making love with him. Life with the alpha grew more rewarding each day.

"Where are you going in such a hurry?" I finally asked, after he'd pulled pants and a t-shirt on, concealing my favorite parts.

He ran his fingers through his hair and walked out of the bathroom with a toothbrush hanging from his mouth, talking around it. "We have a wedding to set in motion. Molly, Tianna, and Sabine are waiting to help you pick out a dress, and Haru, Reo, Cass, and Ray are waiting in the wings to help with whatever else we need. I thought we might get married here, on the land that's been so important to both of our ancestors."

Moving to rinse his mouth, when he returned he sat on the bed next to me and took my hand, looking down at the engagement ring I hadn't removed since I put it on there, right before Caleb's birth. "What do you think of all that? Would you like to get married here? The ceremony could take place next to the creek behind Belinda's cabin."

I sat up and wove my fingers through his. "I think that will be perfect. I really just want to marry you, Brock. I don't need all the fancy stuff."

"That's what you say now." Delight twinkled through his eyes. "Just wait till you see everything the girls have prepared to show you. I think you're going to love it. But obviously, it's whatever you want. Whatever you want to do, I'll be happy. I just want to marry you."

I opened my mouth to say something, but Brock captured my lips in his, and whatever I'd been about to say whisked from my mind, and suddenly I wanted to marry Brock with desperation, like yesterday.

Weaving my hands into his thick hair, I pulled him back into bed with me. As expected, he didn't resist, his hands spreading all across my body in that way of his, where he somehow seemed to touch me everywhere at once.

He slid my thin camisole over my head and immediately brought his tongue to my nipples, banishing all rational thought in an instant. When his fingers skimmed beneath the waistband of my sleep shorts, and he began to slide them down, my own hands went to work, and I had him naked by the time he returned the favor.

"What about the wedding planning?" I asked against his lips, already breathless.

"Everything else can wait. This is what I want. This is what I've always wanted."

Thank God Caleb had moved into his nursery a few months ago.

Moving directly over me, Brock kissed me with enough passion and desire to make my knees go weak. I spread my legs and pulled him down against me, closing my eyes in preparation for the intense pleasure I knew was about to arrive.

And then a baby's shrill cry over the baby monitor filled our bedroom.

We both groaned, and Brock rolled off of me. "Everything else can wait ... but Caleb," Brock said.

"Everything but Caleb," I affirmed, already tugging my sleep clothes back on. Like his parents, Caleb lacked patience, and his crying would only get louder if one of us didn't attend to him right away. I sighed, reached over to lower the volume on the baby monitor, and got out of bed.

The handle to our bedroom door in my hand, I looked

back at Brock over my shoulder. With his hair mussed, and his clothes pulled back on in a rush, he looked delectable. "As soon as I settle Caleb, I'll start approving and setting up wedding stuff. You figure out an exotic honeymoon spot, where we won't have neighbors and I can scream in ecstasy all I want."

Brock's face split into an eager grin. "You got it, baby. I'm thinking white sandy beaches and lots of naked time. Uncle Cass and Aunt Tianna can babysit."

"You read my mind." Winking at him, I slipped through the door, padding toward the nursery next door.

Brock and I were going to get married! I indulged in a giddy smile while no one was looking, and then allowed my heart to melt all over again when I saw our son. A balanced mixture of Brock's features and mine, though he'd inherited my violet eyes, he was beautiful.

When he noticed me, he stopped crying, smiling instead. He stretched his arms out to me and I rushed to pick him up, pressing him against my chest like the miracle that he was.

Who would've thought a one night stand with Brock the Cock could work out so well? I'd gotten everything I hadn't realized I wanted...

Brock had built my father a cabin on the property, where he stayed with Cho, and Molly had settled into Gran's cabin, along with Haru and Reo. Though the warrior brothers mentioned returning to Japan every once in a while, their mentions had become increasingly less frequent as time passed. Tianna had moved in with Cass at his downtown loft, and together he and I trained Molly to become a full-fledged supernatural bounty hunter. Since Molly couldn't leave the area while she was our apprentice, Haru and Reo remained with her. Whatever arrangement the brothers and Molly had, they all seemed happy and in love. It was good enough for me.

The cantankerous old witch Willemena had traveled from her home in California for the wedding, and even Croft and the Blacks had accepted my invitation. I wasn't exactly friends with my mother's family, but after what we'd been through together, it was easier to accept them, though there was still no way in hell I was ever going to bring Caleb around to visit them. I'd been keeping my end of the bargain, visiting Johnny and Aunt Bertie every couple of weeks for a short while, but I'd left Caleb at home every time.

When we added in the hundred or so members of the pack, our wedding had quickly gone from small and intimate to raucous and wild. It suited me just fine.

Brock and I had written our own vows and we'd spoken them to each other beside the trickling creek that ran behind Gran's cabin while Willemena officiated the ceremony. It had been my way of bringing the woman who'd raised me into one of the most important days of my life. There'd been a few times when a breeze had blown just right, delivering the scents of Gran to me, and I'd known that wherever she was, there was a part of her that was watching on.

"Hey, Evie!" Molly hollered across the clearing in the dusk of the balmy night. "Come dance with us!"

Hundreds of lanterns lit by Tianna's magic adorned the forest clearing, and little sparkling lights hung from every tree within sight. The evening was magical, and that was before every person in the world I cared about had gathered to celebrate my union with Brock.

"Maybe in a little bit," I called back to my apprentice, smiling at the way she danced like she owned the night. Haru and Reo trailed every one of her movements with appreciative gazes, taking turns dancing with her. Her purple hair had mostly fallen out of its up-do, but Molly didn't care in the least. She'd make a fabulous bounty hunter, especially since even at the party she wore a handgun strapped to her thigh—just in case. She was taking to her new role as wolf just fine as well. Brock said she was a strong member of the pack.

"I think Molly's had a bit too much to drink," Brock said, leaning into me, sitting on the chair next to me, Caleb on his lap.

I chuckled. "I think everyone here has had too much to drink. They're all happier than I've ever seen them."

"And you?"

"And me what? Am I drunk?"

"No, are you happy?" he asked, amber eyes suddenly serious as they held mine.

I looked from him to our son and back. "I'm happier than I ever thought possible."

His eyes misted and he squeezed one of my hands. "Good. Because so am I."

He leaned over to kiss me, and the moment our lips met, the tinkling of wine goblets rose all around us. I laughed and yelled out, "You're supposed to do that *before* we kiss, to get us to kiss, not after."

"You guys don't need help to kiss," Tianna hollered.

"And neither do we," Cass said, sidling up to his

Amazonian fae-witch, wrapping an arm around one of her thighs beneath her short dress. Cass had ordered a special set of rhinestone booty shorts for the event; he wore them and a matching rhinestone-studded bow tie. He looked like a Chippendale dancer, if the male strippers were short and pot-bellied. Regardless, as usual, Cass rocked the look, and of everyone at the party he was smiling the most.

"My girl," he crooned, claiming the chair next to mine and wrapping a short, stubby arm around the back of it. "I never thought I'd see the day you'd be married with a baby. But you're rocking it like you've rocked everything else in your life. You're a fine bride, and a finer mother. I couldn't be prouder of you."

"Shit, Cass. You can't make me cry at my own wedding reception," I whispered, swiping beneath my eyes to keep my mascara from running down my cheeks.

"You know me," he said, "I gotta speak my heart with you. Always have."

I nodded. "I love you too, Cass. Best friends forever."

"Forever," he echoed, and took in Brock and Caleb. "You take good care of my girl, Brock. I know where to find you if you don't."

Brock smirked. "That's because you live five minutes away and have a telepathic connection with my wife."

My wife. My breath hitched in my chest as emotion rushed through me, and I blinked furiously, trying to keep myself together.

"Still," Cass pressed, "you know I'll always have her back."

"Cass, my friend," Brock said, "I wouldn't have it any

other way. For Evie, everything. I'd give her the entire world if I could."

"You already did," I squeaked, and Brock and Cass both whirled on me as I sniffled. But they didn't comment on my emotional moment. Cass leaned his head against my shoulder, and Brock squeezed my thigh beneath my dress.

"What do you say I get out of this dress and we head off on our next adventure?" I asked Brock.

He grinned. "Getting you out of this dress has been top on my list all night."

Cass chuckled. "Finally, my girl's getting as much action as I am."

Before Cass could elaborate, I shot to my feet, picking up Caleb. "I'll change. If you can grab our bags, we can leave right after," I told Brock.

"The happy couple is leaving for their honeymoon!" Cass announced the second I stopped talking. "Let's gather round to see them off so they can go have lots and lots of hot sex!"

The wolf pack threw their heads back and howled into the descending night. I laughed, working to ignore the fact that my dad was out there among them somewhere.

"Cass might be drunk," Brock commented, but I wasn't sure. Sex was always Cass' favorite topic and he knew he had to babysit, so he'd better not be.

By the time I returned in my signature tight jeans, crop top, and kickass boots, everyone had gathered, and they were cheering, hooting and hollering, basically making as much noise as you might imagine a hundred-plus-odd supes could make.

Brock stood at his truck, our bags loaded, "Just

married" scrawled across every window except the windshield. Silently, he extended his hand toward me, and wolves and witches whistled and yelled some more.

"Evie..."

The one word had me searching for the one person I wanted to be sure I saw before I left. "Dad..."

The crowd parted so he could wheel forward, Cho pushing him along the rough terrain of Brock's land—of *our* land—until he was close enough to continue on his own.

"I'm so proud of you, my daughter. You're strong and magical and beautiful, inside and out. You're fit to lead these people who surround you."

"This is Brock's pack, not mine," I answered my dad. "He will be leading them, not me."

My dad shook his head gently, his dark hair sliding along his head. "Now that you're married, what's his is yours, and these wolves look up to you already. I have no doubt you'll prove a fit leader."

I opened my mouth to say something, but shut it in the end, and simply nodded and smiled.

"Your mother would have been just as proud of you as I am," he added, and I sniffled.

"Thanks, Dad," I said over that pesky lump in my throat.

"Now, go have some fun with your husband. You've earned it."

I tried not to consider what he might be suggesting, especially with Cass and Tianna laying on the sexual innuendo as thick as icing on a cake for their eager audience. Nodding rapidly, I stepped to Brock instead.

"Say goodbye to Daddy," I told Caleb while Brock leaned down to kiss our son's forehead.

"Come to Uncle Cass." My bestie was approaching us, his hands outstretched.

"You're sure you can handle him while we're gone?" I asked.

Cass brought both stubby hands to his hips, bringing my full attention to his rhinestone booty shorts. It seemed as if every single light in the forest reflected off his attire. "Of course I can handle him. If I can take down giant trolls and demons, I can surely handle a little rug-rat for a few days. He and I are going to have so much fun. I have the whole week planned out. We'll hit the bar every night to pick up the fae ladies."

Suddenly Tianna was right behind Cass, her arms crossed, a scowl pressed across her face. He hip-bumped her. "You know I'm just kidding, T. The fae ladies are for the little man, not me."

I panicked. "The 'little man' does not need to be going to bars. Maybe this was a mistake."

Cass laughed, clutched his little potbelly, and then he laughed some more. "I'm just messing with ya, Eve. We've got it under control. I even bought this little baby piano for him to play with. Go have fun. T and Molly are going to help me."

I glanced at Molly. She was drinking straight from a bottle of wine, dancing with both brothers at the same time, one pressed to either side of her, their hands all over her.

Cass peered at her too. "She'll help me tomorrow. Once she sleeps off her hangover."

"Come on, wife, you heard Cass. Time to have some

adult fun." Brock kissed Caleb another time, took him from me, and handed him over to Cass, who promptly hitched my baby boy onto his rhinestoned hip. Caleb was instantly fascinated with the lightshow that was Cass, playing with his sparkly bowtie. In another three years my son would by taller than my bestie.

"He'll be fine," Brock whispered, his breath hot in my ear. "We need time for ourselves."

Hell yeah we did. I nodded, my eyes pinned to Caleb, and allowed Brock to lead me to the truck.

After our guests supplied enough fanfare to make me feel like a celebrity, Brock finally pulled the truck away, beeping the horn lightly a few times. Even with the windows closed, I could make out the celebration of those we were leaving behind.

Brock pointed us away from home and started down the long drive toward town, and eventually the airport.

"So where are we going?" I asked.

"I booked us a very private hut directly over the crystal-clear water in French Polynesia. There will be plenty of fine white sand, sunshine, and no clothes required. Hell, better yet, no clothes allowed. How's that sound?"

"Like a dream."

Wild sex with a naked Brock, with no crying baby. What more could this girl ask for?

I'd already gotten everything I wanted.

READ MORE BY THE AUTHORS

Evie's story has drawn to an end, but if you enjoyed her adventures, check out another of Lucía and Leia's series! They all contain plenty of magic, adventure, and attitude.

Find your next read:

Lucía's Amazon page:
http://www.amazon.com/author/luciaashta
Leia's Amazon page:
https://www.amazon.com/Leia-Stone/e/BooKBXMBDA
Lucía's webpage:
https://www.luciaashta.com
Leia's webpage:
https://leiastone.com

To learn about all the fun stuff they're up to:

Sign up for Lucía's newsletter:
https://www.subscribepage.com/luciaashta

Join Lucía's Facebook reader group:
https://www.facebook.com/groups/LuciaAshta
Follow Lucía on Facebook:
https://www.facebook.com/authorluciaashta
Sign up for Leia's monthly newsletter:
https://leiastone.com/newsletter/
Follow Leia on Facebook:
https://www.facebook.com/leia.stone/

Thank you for reading our wild stories!

ACKNOWLEDGMENTS FROM LEIA

Wow what a fun Co-authoring experience. A big thank you to Lucia for being an amazing, creative, and easygoing individual.

Thank you to our editor Lee from Ocean's Edge editing for putting the finishing touches on this manuscript. Also a huge thanks to our ARC team for their excitement for this book and for helping find any last typos. Lastly, thank you to my family as always for supporting my dream. Love you guys.

Oh and I can't forget, thank you Tate James for teaching me what a crotch goblin is.

ACKNOWLEDGMENTS FROM LUCÍA

A huge thank you to Leia for having faith in our seed of an idea, which led to the adventures you just read. I didn't realize it could be so much fun to share a fictional world with another writer! Of course, Leia is no ordinary author. In her, I found not only a fabulous writer, but also a wonderful friend. Leia, I'm ever so grateful to share this wild ride with you, girl.

I'm also deeply thankful to all the readers who make the endless hours working on our books worthwhile. Creating magical worlds is a great passion of mine, one which would be far less meaningful without your support. Thank you, dear readers, for all your enthusiasm and love for our characters! It means the world to me.

And finally, a great big goofy-smile thank you to my family. My three daughters, beloved, and mother are there for me through the ups and downs, and they love me through it all. I'm so grateful that you believe in me and the crazy ideas I come up with. I love you!

Made in the USA
Middletown, DE
06 February 2020